The Intersection

Catherine Grace

This paperback edition published 2020 by Jasami Publishing Ltd
an imprint of Jasami Publishing Ltd
Glasgow, Scotland
https://jasamipublishingltd.com

ISBN 978-1-913798-03-1

Visit JasamiPublishingLtd.com to read more about all our books and to purchase them. You will also find features, author information and news of any events, also be the first to hear about our new releases.

Acknowledgements

I must acknowledge Glasgow.
The city that has been home to me all my life, even when I lived
thousands of miles away.

Fine Art Photographer - Cover
John McIntosh

Creative Editor
Paula A Weir

Editor
Edward Doyle

May Winton
You are extraordinary

&

Finally,
Without you I would never have found
My Intersection

Dedication

This book is dedicated to my Mum and Dad
I miss you both every day.

May mystery always enthrall you.

Cath Grace.

Table of Contents

Prologue

*I*t was a rainy day in the cemetery, worthy of any movie scene. The small, solitary shadow dressed in the black of mourning was the lone figure left after the ceremony, which had been small, the only attendees were the minister and herself. She wanted it that way. She dropped a single long-stemmed red rose on top of the casket and her tears mingled with the rain.

"I will honour your memory," she whispered. "You will not be forgotten."

She straightened her slender frame, and drew in a ragged breath, the agony in her heart was like a physical stabbing pain, leaving behind a black hole. She nodded her head knowing exactly what she would do.

Chapter One

A nd so the story begins.

Em rolled her eyes and wished for the days of typewriters, when she could easily have pulled out the paper, scrunched it into a paper ball, and imitating the American basketball players, throw it across the room, quite often making the basket in the corner. Metaphoric, but it relieved the frustration of the moment.

She viewed the sentence and wondered exactly how many clichés were permissible in a story. Closing her eyes, she pressed the delete key until she heard the beep beep beep, indicating that it was objecting to any more deletions.

That's it she thought, "I need inspiration! I shall view My Intersection.

She left her small office and went into the front hallway. She remembered selecting just the right shade for the mahogany flooring to compliment the rich vibrant colours of the woven carpets. She clicked on the kitchen light to offset the early sunset of a Glasgow winter. She followed the same ritual, boiling the kettle, putting three teabags into the teapot to let it steep and become as black as coal. Maria had left a small pile of fresh-made gooey chocolate chip cookies and Em prudently placed only two onto the small china plate. She pulled the tray from the tall cupboard and neatly organised the teapot, cup, saucer, teaspoon, napkin, and cookies for easy carrying. This simple ritual always calmed her and she smiled as she walked into the front lounge and placed the laden tray on the table.

Em loved the view from the fourth-floor large bay window so common to the architecture of Roberts Street. She snuggled into the overstuffed wing chair and pulled the tartan woollen wrap loosely around her shoulders, the tea and treats within easy reach. She glanced at the clock over the fireplace, noting it was getting close to six o'clock so her intersection would be fairly busy with people homeward bound. Em bit into the still-warm cookie, sipped the piping hot tea and was thankful she was not out on this winter's night. The snow from this morning's fall was settling into white trails and grey mush on the street. Smiling to herself she continued to sip her tea and watch the familiar train of people walking home from work. Mr. Benedict who lived around the corner looked up and waved, his red gloves, scarf, and hat almost glowing in the streetlight, Em raised her cup in a silent toast and bit into the last of her chocolate chip cookies. A few minutes later she watched as the twins walked through the intersection, passed in front of her building and walked further down the road before entering the close at the end. Their white-blonde hair, California beach tan and model figures were incongruous with their surroundings which usually caused heads to turn, and in some cases, almost swivel around as they passed.

The darkness of the room was broken only slightly by the faint glow of her laptop, as she contemplated a return to work on her short story before the buzzing of her mobile phone interrupted.

"Hi, Sarah."

"Hey Em, what's going on in the neighbourhood? How's life in your favourite intersection?"

"No," she groaned, "please do not tell me I am that predictable?"

"Yes, you are and you know it! It's about 6:30 pm and if I know, you've had tea and cookies."

"Anyway, Sarah to answer your question no it's not so busy tonight, just a few going home, and of course the twins. Maybe the cold is keeping everybody inside."

"In Glasgow! I don't think so. You know that they go out in a summer dress even in the middle of winter! Remember that time we watched those girls teetering home at four in the morning? Each one hanging on to the other and not one winter coat between them?"

"Sarah, they had the alcohol to keep them warm. And now to more important things, what can I do for you?"

"Ah, it's more what can I do for you!" Sarah paused for effect then continued, "I've got wine and steak and asparagus and potatoes and key lime pie, listing off one Emily's favourite dinners.

"The only thing I don't have Em is a lovely bottle of red, I don't suppose that you might have one?"

Em laughed, she always had wine but there was little food in the house, so she agreed to have dinner made for her as she wondered what the required payment would be. Maybe a review of a paper? Or finances? Sarah was a brilliant painter and in demand. She had both an accountant and an agent, yet still always came to Em first for her review of any business issues. Whatever it was, Em was happy to do since it meant she would have company for an evening and not even have to cook.

A quick view of the flat assured Em it was ready for a friend, not a guest, someone who didn't require pristine.

Em loved her flat, it had been built in the 1870s and was a vivid red sandstone, this area was awash with colour as one street over the buildings were constructed of yellow sandstone. The building was solid, although Em remembered Peter telling her the story of the tragedy that happened only two streets over. It was around the same time her flat was built, but the other building collapsed killing six workers. Incredibly no one had noticed that it was being constructed on landfill. Em shivered, not from the cold, but from the sadness of unnecessary death, and then felt a tear slide down her cheek, death, tragedy, it was always the same it made her think of Peter.

The buzzer intruded on her tears and she quickly wiped them away before answering the door for her closest friend.

Sarah sailed through the door with her arms full of packages while dictating. "You open the wine Em and I'll start the dinner, and I'll tell you all about my day and just how mad some clients can be."

Sarah chatted on about mad clients as she moved about the immaculate kitchen. The kitchen was laid out in a rectangular shape with a surround of black granite and natural wood made from knotty pine. There was an island worktop in the centre with black leather barstools around three sides with the open side next to the sink and stove. Stained glass framed a large plain glass window which allowed perfect viewing of the back garden, that was actually a common area enclosed by the four buildings. It resembled a small park rather than a typical garden and each neighbour was very serious about the care and feeding of the grounds. Two large English oaks were the prey of the tree climbing children while the alder trees provided shade for a few avid gardeners who kept the area awash with colour during the summer. Another overstuffed chair provided a perfect viewing spot for Em.

Em settled on one of the barstools, sipping the rich California Zinfandel and smiled in amazement at the energy of her petite friend as Sarah darted from stove to cupboards with the speed of a hummingbird. Twenty minutes, and a glass of wine, later they were at the dining table, lit only by white pillar candles and the large fireplace.

"To new adventures." Sarah smiled as she raised her wine to toast.

"To new adventures." chimed Em then enquired, "what adventure is it this time?"

Sarah took a moment to fill her fork and pop it into her mouth to consider before answering.

"Well, I'm off to California for a few weeks to do a new commission, Gray and Alisa want an ocean series done, and, well I thought that it would be great if you would come and keep me company and we could shop and visit the Fishery and the Market and...." the speed of the words had continued to increase until Sarah's voice died off, seeing Em's expression.

Em put down her knife and fork then lacing her fingers together she rested her chin to gaze sadly before saying, "Sarah, you of all people, know I can't go."

"But?"

"No!" her voice broke. "You know I can't, I just can't."

Em pushed her chair back from the table, stood and turned away, towards the window, to the intersection, her intersection, and the street life she so loved to watch from the safety of her home.

Em repeated. "I'm sorry Sarah. I just can't."

Em leaned her head against the window not even trying to stop the flow of tears or the memories.

"Peter what are you doing with that disgusting hat?"

Emily Lawson, one of the youngest graduates from the University of Southern California, looked at her new husband with a mixture of love and disgust.

Peter Sullivan, the young professor on sabbatical from Glasgow University, returned the look of reproach with a wide mischievous smile, and grabbed his wife of three months, tickling her middle and proceeded to plant the offending hat onto her head, the old-fashioned Trilby hat that somehow had accumulated dried bits of twig, dirt and a sticky web tangled into the mass of long curly blonde hair, producing the expected shriek followed by giggles, then followed by slow sweet kisses.

An hour later, wet from the shower the pair surveyed each other with the same loving look that had become common over the last year.

"How about pizza?" he asked, "before we continue packing up this mess you call your life."

Pouting she retorted, "I'd prefer ice cream..." she hesitated, and then "with anchovies."

"Ugh! that takes your weird food taste to a whole new level."

Em smiled, "Well yes... but there is a reason for that."
She pulled him into her arms and whispered.

Chapter Two

❚❚ Em turned over in her large lonely bed and opened one blue eye to peer out of the window. At nine in the morning, the clouds covered the sky and the black threatened another winter storm.

The phone buzzed.

Em groaned.

Pulling on an oversized woollen sweater Em padded barefoot into her gleaming kitchen, mentally listing her priorities, coffee first order of the day, shower the second, breakfast, and only then answer the phone.

As if on cue the front door buzzed, and a sleepy slightly grumpy Em answered the door and then allowed a small smile as she greeted the red-headed youth.

"Hi Mrs. Lawson, how are you today?" Tommy grinned his familiar, slightly crooked toothy smile while holding out the bag containing her daily order of freshly baked morning rolls, bacon, two scones, fresh cream as well as the morning paper.

"Hi Tommy," Em's smiled widened in return, causing the normal rush of red to mix with the freckles on Tommy's young face and matching his ginger hair.

"How is maths?" Em enquired about the only subject Tommy had problems with.

"It's okay," Tommy blushed and grinned again.

"Yes?"

"I got a 2a on my exam."

"Excellent!" exclaimed Em, raising her hand and slapping Tommy's in a high five.

"Well, .Mrs. Lawson, I was wondering if we could start that game you were talking about?"

"Of course, Tommy. Your reward will be Chess and High tea this afternoon, as I will need additional supplies today."

Once the order had been placed and the time arranged, Em scurried to the kitchen to pour coffee, spread butter and blackcurrant jam on a roll, and head into the front lounge and her favourite bay window to survey life in her intersection. Em usually referred to it as her intersection as she felt a bond with the neighbourhood that went beyond normal interest, it was her way to live life on the outside without ever having to go out into the world that had taken so much from her. She knew if she stayed safe inside she would not feel the loss, the devastating pain that engulfed the outside world.

Her world was her flat which consisted of eight rooms, running front to back on the right side of the building located on the top floor. Along the back of the building ran the kitchen, a guest bedroom and bathroom and a bedroom converted into a closet. Along the front of the building were the living room and front lounge, the master bedroom with an adjoining bedroom which had been converted, during the renovation into a marble bathroom that would have rivalled the Romans' idea of decadence.

The entire room was constructed of pale cream marble with a toilet and bidet hidden in the corner behind a half wall. On the right side was an L shaped walk-in shower, and nearer to the door was the dressing area, and a built-in marble vanity, while square mirrors alternated with the marble in the vanity to create a disconnected reflection.

The entire flat had the wood floors refinished and brought back to their original life, and was warmed with Chinese rugs, Scottish tapestries, and original oil paintings courtesy of Sarah. Candlelight bathed every room while the individual and unique colour of each room reflected the warmth and variance of Em's personality.

Em sipped the last dregs of coffee and licked her finger. She had missed the morning regulars and those who passed on the street now were day-to-day strangers who never touched her life.

At that moment her eyes opened wide. The turn of the head, the curly black hair and the width of the shoulders. It couldn't be! It absolutely could not be! So once again the memories invaded.

Peter pulled Em back and looked into her eyes and then scooped her up and twirled her around the room until they were both dizzy and falling once more onto the bed.

"Are you sure?"

Em smiled and nodded, pulling Peter close, "Absolutely and positively."

"Well, are you sure the move is a good idea? Should we wait? Do you want to wait? I mean—"

"Peter will you stop!" Em interrupted gently placing a finger across his lips. "I'm healthy and everything is wonderful. We're going back to Glasgow, to your home and our child will be born there and life will be what we make of it, which as long as we are together will be perfection."

Em smiled warm and safe in his arms, not knowing just how wrong she would be.

"I'm coming, I'm coming," Em spoke loudly as the knocking continued.

Pulling the door open wide she saw the welcome sight of her blond bear-sized neighbour, who wasted no time pulling her into a hug.

"I missed you!" Stefan exclaimed, pushing Em away to examine her face and then pulling her into his warm embrace again. Em waved back and forth like a willow tree, feeling the familiar warmth of his arms.

"Stefan you've only been gone two weeks!"

"Feels like two years, and what does a guy have to do around here to get a cup of tea?"

Em smiled against his chest replying in a muffled voice, "it would help if I was in the kitchen and had free arms to put on the kettle"

"Humph" he grumbled, letting her go.

Since Em moved into the flat three years ago Stefan had decided that he was her guardian angel and best friend and no amount of arguing or rationalising could change his mind.

Walking past her he lifted his arm so it cleared her head and proceeded directly into the kitchen to put the kettle on with Em following along.

"May I have tea too?"

"It's your place don't see why not," Stefan smiled, offering her a tall stool and turning to produce mugs, plates, scones, butter and jam, as was the ritual when he returned from time away on one of his photographic shoots.

"So did you fall in love with any beautiful models this time?" Em teased, knowing full well the answer.

"Oh yes about a dozen or so," Stefan winked.

At six feet three inches his Nordic ancestry showed in his blond blue-eyed features, his large well-build frame reminded Em of rugby players, and she tried to remember if he said that he had ever played.

Em knew he had no shortlist of the women he dated, but in all the time she had known him he had never had a long-term relationship. It was one of those few subjects that they had mutually agreed that it would never be discussed.

"So what have you written since I've been gone?" Stefan seemed to track Em's writing assignments better than she did.

Em groaned. "Two short Christmas murder mysteries but it's the teen Christmas story that's due in a few days which I haven't started yet, I mean I tried, but ending up deleting it all."

He raised an eyebrow and waggled his forefinger while shaking his head.

"And it's not what you think," Em said, answering the gesture before the question even came out.

"I started it and… well, I kind of started it… okay okay! I got one line out 'and so begins the story' I mean, how silly is that? All I was doing was thinking in clichés, completely and totally idiotic!"

Stefan served the tea and pulled up a chair next to Em.

"What's it supposed to be about? And can't Tommy give you some insight? You know it would make his year to help you out." Stefan winked again, to emphasise his teasing Em about the crush that Tommy so obviously displayed.

Em rolled her eyes, and then they discussed different ideas for the story. Soon after they finished Em started to clear up the dishes and paused in thought.

"What is it? I can see your mind creating steam from thinking so hard."

"Stefan, you know Sarah's going to California for a few weeks, but she's still going to be here for my Christmas party. How about a celebratory dinner here?"

"Sounds great, as long as you promise that you're not still trying to fix us up. It didn't work the first time," commented Stefan, remembering when Em tried to bring them together in a feeble matchmaking attempt, and several thereafter.

Raising her right hand Em promised.

"Fine." said Stefan rising from the stool and kissing her forehead. "I've got to process some film - I know can you believe it? Not everything is digital?"

He scratched his head. "How about dinner?"

Em nodded

"There's a new Bistro around the corner—" he began.

Em furiously shook her head, "What is it with you two? Sarah tried the same thing last night! No, and especially not now!" and before he could question her she continued, "how about I make steak pie and potatoes here?"

He shrugged, "Just thought…"

"And I think you're wonderful, but it's so lovely at home."

"One day Em you'll have to go out. It's not right the way you…"

"Don't start Stefan," interrupted Em, her sapphire eyes narrowing, the first sign of her stubborn resolution.

He held up his hands in surrender and once again bent to brush her forehead with his lips.

"See you later."

Em smiled, shut the door, and after a quick clean-up in the kitchen returned to the lounge and to the familiar spot at the window to watch life out on the intersection.

The lives that walked, strolled, cycled and drove by fascinated her. There was old Mrs. McLean who lived in the flat directly across the street and walked her pet every day, a bad tempered sleek white cat that wore a bright pink sparkling necklace attached to a matching fuchsia leash. The normal ritual was to carry Snowball down the stairs place her on the pavement then proceed down the street often stopping to gently pull rather than drag the lead. Em fashioned lives of the people she did not know and would often use them in the stories she created in her freelance writing work.

Imagining their lives is so much easier than living my own, she often thought. As she gazed out the window her eye's clouded over with a memory.

"Mrs. Lawson?" The tall policeman leaned to the right to block out the brilliant California sunshine of the early afternoon. The squint of Em's eyes eased.

"Yes officer, how can I help?"

"I'm sorry ma'am, may we have a moment?"

"Yes?"

"I'm afraid there's been an accident at the university and your husband…"

"Peter?" Em whispered the word, then her voice grew stronger. "Well, what hospital is he in? What happened? How bad are his injuries?" Her

14

voice then faded as she watched the expression that was to remain stoic, soften with emotion.

She remembered hearing the ocean in her head and then nothing.

It was a day later before she woke up. Peter had died in the accident, and she had been in the hospital recovering from the miscarriage.

Chapter Three

"Good morning Mrs.. Lawson," Tommy smiled and his face infused in the usual red as Em smiled in return.

"Morning Tommy and how is maths treating you today?" The familiar question bringing a wider smile.

"It's good. I've been working with my tutor and it's getting easier." Tommy shuffled his feet side to side, the asked "Mrs. Lawson?"

"Yes, Tommy? Em stepped back to give Tommy room for the extra groceries ordered for the small Christmas party that evening.

"Do you know someone with black curly hair?"

Em raised her eyebrows in question.

"I mean, do you know someone who you think you might know, but aren't sure because they aren't sure if they know you, and you might know each other but not know it?"

"What!?"

Tommy sputtered and stuttered and then the words came out in a rush, as was common when he was nervous or upset. "Well the other day I was bringing your stuff up and this man asked if I knew the pretty lady with the long curly hair who watches everyone at the window, and I said I knew a pretty lady with long curly hair but that I didn't know that you watched at the window and —"

"Tommy! What are you talking about?" Em lost patience as one of the bags broke and oranges spilt across the floor.

Then looking up and seeing Tommy's stricken face she relented.

"I know lot's of people, you know, and some have curly black hair–" Em stopped short.

Her heart thumped against her chest. The most beautiful black curly hair belonged to Peter and hadn't she seen someone exactly like that just the other day? But she had dismissed it as imagination.

Dropping the bags, Em took Tommy by the hand and sat him on the chair in the hall.

"Now Tommy think very, very carefully. What did this man look like?"

Tommy screwed up his blue eyes and scratched his wiry ginger hair.

"Well he kinda looked like a pirate with smooth skin and brown eyes and black hair, and he had a nice smile, I mean his teeth were straight, not crooked like you would expect a pirate to have, even though I said that he looked like a pirate he wasn't dressed like one. I mean he looked like the pirate in the movie except for his teeth..." Tommy's description faded as he watched Em's face.

It couldn't be. It just couldn't. Peter had been dead for just over three years, and once again the memories flooded in.

Sarah had come, flown in from New York, and flitted around the hospital taking charge. It was one loss too many.

The next few days were just a jumble of blue skies, black limousines, people pressing their hands into her's offering heartfelt but useless words of regret. They didn't understand Peter and the baby were both her entire world and they had both died, the hole was unfillable.

Sarah hadn't pressed her about what Em would do, but Em knew all along what she would do. She would stick to the plan that Peter and she had made. Return to Glasgow, to his home, to the flat he had bought and wanted to renovate and make into their home. And that is just what she did. She meticulously followed the plan and renovated the flat strictly according to Peter's design, not changing one tiny detail, and when it was complete, she knew that she had come home, and the best part was she would never have to leave.

Chapter Four

" Em I've already done my shopping and I don't need any oranges," Stefan's voice interrupted the questioning.

Standing in the doorway with four of the oranges he promptly began to juggle creating a distraction for Tommy and his quick exit.

"What are you doing to scare the child?" began Stefan, and then seeing Em's face immediately led her into the lounge pouring a strong brandy.

"I'm fine, I'm fine. Really I am," Em assured Stefan. "It's just..." she hesitated. She rarely discussed Peter, even with Stefan.

"Does it have to do with Peter?" he asked reading her mind.

"What makes you think that?

"I rarely see you ruffled, even though you're cooped up in here all the time, and I know how private that subject is to you."

"Well, yes," Em answered and quickly related what Tommy had told her.

Stefan looked up from his squatting position on the floor looking into Em's eyes.

"So what do you think it is? Peter reincarnated? Or someone who just happens to look like him?"

Em rolled her eyes as she realised how silly she was jumping to the conclusion it was Peter, and how it must sound when she was speaking to an intelligent and caring adult.

"Okay I'm a silly girl... it's just...well I guess if I had a chance to believe that he wasn't dead I would."

Stefan hesitated.

"Yes?" asked Em.

"Nothing," replied Stefan smiling and with her hands in his gently pulled her to her feet, although the smile did not quite reach his eyes, which only showed concern.

"Tell me, what are you planning to do with these oranges? Your Christmas party looms and here you sit dilly-dallying away the day."

Chapter Five

*T*he front lounge of 224 Roberts Street glittered with all the colours of Christmas. The centre of the room had been cleared and the rich reds and greens of the Chinese rugs were the focal point. Garlands hung in loops, and cream coloured pillar candles provided the dancing lights. Silhouetted against one side of the front bay window stood a lush Fraser Fir Christmas tree artistically decorated and topped with an angel dressed in cream with wings made of small willowy feathers.

Sarah flitted from one guest to another, looking angelic in a floaty white chiffon evening dress which swirled and followed her around the room like an ardent admirer. Her short black curly hair framed her tiny face and the red of her lipstick was the only colour she wore.

Em wore a burgundy velvet dress that clung to her, accentuating her willowy curves. Her long curly blonde hair was pulled up on one side and cascaded down the other in a mass of golden curls.

Stefan conceded to Em's wishes to shave his short-cropped beard and wore the navy silk suit with the tie as requested, despite his protestations.

The room filled with friends, colleagues and a few neighbours: Em's publisher Roger Egbert and his trophy wife Miranda, Em's accountant Mary Louise Smith and her husband Jared, Tommy, his younger sister and their parent's John and Ethel Witherspoon, Mrs. McLean of the eccentric cat walking duties, and Mr. Brown from around the corner attired in his normal brown suit, his only concession to Christmas being the garish seasonal tie.

Before this party, Tommy had only been as far as the hallway and so he wandered around examining the details of Em's life. Egyptian paintings portraying the lives of pharaohs and those who honoured them in vivid colours of blue, blazing white, red, gold and copper all with the characteristic toes facing the Pharaoh.

"Wow!" Tommy sighed, stopping at the elaborate chess set showcased next to the Christmas tree. Made of pewter all the pieces represented magical wizards, the king adorned with a staff topped with an iridescent globe, the sorceress queen with small emeralds encircling her neck, indeed each pewter piece contained a small glittering object.

Em leaned towards Tommy. "Do you remember I promised you a game?"

Tommy, blushing as usual, raised his eyes. "Yep," he said, picking up his second favourite Americanism, nope being his first.

"When would you like to begin?" Em smiled and sat on the small stool at the white side of the board.

"Soon, ohh that would be soooooooooooo great, I'd know something I didn't before, and I could teach the guys at school and we could play, and I would—." He stopped suddenly, catching Em's eye.

"You know," she said, "it's a thinking man's game," quickly adding "women too. Not a lot of talking, just thinking and strategising. I'll tell you what," she continued, "since you're off school for the next few weeks, when you drop off my messages, if okay with Mum and Dad, of course, we could have some starter games. How would you like that?"

Tommy smiled and gave a big thumbs up, which had to be the quickest and quietest assent Em had ever witnessed.

She winked at Ethel, Tommy's mum, and returning Tommy's thumbs up she excused herself, walked over to the gesturing Sarah.

"When's dinner?" asked Sarah.

"Why? Are you starved?"

"Not yet, but soon, and that's not what I'm talking about. The doorbell rang and—"

"And you answered it like the good little assistant hostess you are!" Em said, putting her arm around Sarah. "And who was at the door? Santa?"

Sarah pulled gently away, looking up at Em, small furrows wrinkled her smooth forehead.

"I'm not quite sure how to say this."

Stefan interrupted. "Sarah I've never known you to be speechless in your life," he teased handing Em a glass of sauvignon blanc and offering one to Sarah.

Em smiled her thanks at Stefan.

"Thanks, Stefan but I don't want a glass of wine right now." Sarah turned back to Em and her large chocolate brown eyes reflected concern and fear.

Em knew it was a crisis if Sarah refused wine and laughing said so.

"Just stop you two, you're both like a comedy routine without the funny. What I am trying to say is a guy stopped by to see Em, and I didn't like the look of him."

Stefan immediately straightened himself up to his full height making the hall seem quite small. "What's wrong with him?" he asked, "and where is he? I'll take care of it."

"He's gone. I sent him away," Sarah's voice faded then broke. "I'm sorry Em, he just looked so very much like Peter, it was so eerie and weird."

Em swayed towards Stefan but her eyes were wide open. Gripping Sarah's arm, she asked "Are you sure it wasn't him? Maybe?"

"Em! You know it can't be, you know he's...he's dead, he's dead and we both have to—."

Stefan interrupted with an emphatic "Who is he? What does he want?"

Sarah lifted her chin and tilted her head back to look at Em directly, "I'm not sure who he is. He said he was a friend of Peter's and wanted to talk to you. He said he hadn't known that Peter had died until recently and he wanted to offer his condolences."

Em passed her hand across her eyes, remembering when she had looked out over the intersection, and her shock as she had seen the dark curly haired man who looked to be the twin of Peter, the one who had spoken to Tommy, and now wanted to speak to her. Remembering the sight of him caused a physical jolt, he was just so much like Peter, even though it couldn't be him.

Every night for over three years she had wished with all her heart that she could be with Peter, feel his arms around her waist, the scent of him as she pressed her head against his chest, and he would rest his chin on her head, yet every morning she would wake up to face another day without him. Sometimes she would roll out of bed, and sometimes the physical pain of her aching loss would cause her to roll over and sob into the pillow until she was exhausted, and sometimes if she was very lucky she would fall asleep and dream once again of being with him. Then over the last year, ever so slowly, each day was easier to face. The cloudy sky, the grey sky and even the occasional sunny sky that was a Glasgow morning started to bring her to life, and the pain that used to grate like a newly sharpened knife softened to a small stab that caught her breathe.

Em looked at Sarah, inhaled a breath and released it slowly.

"Whoever he is and whatever he wants I will not let this ruin our Christmas." Em looked into Sarah's eyes. "You know how much I love Peter and will always love him, but you are here and I am here and we will live and love and be a part of this madness

24

called life. You are so dear to me——." Em's voice broke as she pulled the tiny Sarah into a hug, and then they were both engulfed in the warm and comforting arms of Stefan.

Tommy's anxious voice broke the spell. "Mrs. Lawson? May I have a candy?"

The trio broke apart to see the freckled face of the red-headed boy who so obviously loved Emily, and they smiled as they went to find the candy that filled every candy dish on every table in the house.

Chapter Six

"Is it possible for me to just remove my head and put it in ice until it feels better?" Em spoke to the air, even though the question was directed at Sarah on the adjacent sofa, who just moaned an answer.

Miraculously the house was in pristine order even though the party had broken up at about two in the morning. This was due entirely to Em's housekeeping guardian angel Maria, who came along with four organised daughters, and who took precisely one hour to scour the house and return it to its usual order.

Maria smiled and bobbed her head. "You take care, you take care now," and ordering her daughters left the flat in short order.

"Is that why they call it Boxing day? Because you feel as if you've been boxing and lost every single round and been beaten to a pulp and have nothing left to live for?" Em once again asked the air, as the only response was a further mumble.

Knowing the right question to ask, Em asked, "What about some tea and chocolate cake?"

The answering mumble turned into an "Mmm..."

Em propped up on one elbow and squinted one eye open and asked herself "Where was winter hiding?" The day after Christmas and the sun was shining , the sky was blue with not a single cloud in sight, as if it were summer in California.

"Enough of this." Em spoke aloud as she swung her legs over the edge of the sofa, her toes searching the floor for slippers, once connected she slipped into the kitchen and set the kettle to boil.

Neat piles of plastic holders showed off the wares of leftovers from the party, one of which was chocolate cake.

Assembling coffee for herself and tea for Sarah, and a large plate piled high with chocolate cake, Em balanced the tray with morning paper under her arm placing them on the coffee table which had been returned to its home between the two black leather sofas.

Once the chocolate cake breakfast had been consumed and washed down with copious cups of coffee and tea, Em broached the subject.

"So what do you think this guy wants?"

Sarah half-opened both eyes. "I don't know. Tell you the truth Em, he looks so much like Peter it's scary. But he's got this weird kind of accent that is, well, *weird*. He looks like Peter but when he opens his mouth this American-Italian accent comes out and it just doesn't figure."

Sarah licked the last of the chocolate from her fingers, in unison with Em.

"Well, if meeting him is what I have to do to figure this out then... Are we blowing this out of proportion? I mean we all have someone who looks like ourselves, this is just that right?" Em asked, wanting more than just an agreement.

"You lost your husband, and I lost my cousin in that explosion," answered Sarah. "We had to face it and deal with it. Just because someone looks like him means.... well, it's just that, it means that there is someone who looks like him, and that's it for me now, my head hurts and I need a nap." Sarah snuggled under the duvet hiding her head so that only a couple of dark curls showed at the top.

"I don't know how you don't suffocate," said Em, before resigning herself to the fact that her dear friend and Peter's only cousin was not to be disturbed.

Chapter Seven

*T*hree *years earlier*.

"He's worth millions ya know? And you can get your fair share."

"It's not really my fair share ya know?" he replied, repeating the slang.

"Yeah I know an makin' fun of me ain't gonna help."

"Sorry."

"Yeah, okay."

"So what is the plan anyway?"

"Well, he's workin' at his lab tonight. Ya can go an have a talk with him, convince him you're his long-lost brother."

"But?"

"But nothing! He gets funny — you just deal with it! Ya know what I mean?"

"Are you sure I look just like him?"

"Brother you're his spittin' image! I've been workin' at that lab for months and he's nice talkin' and stuff but lemme tell ya, you two are identical, so you could be 'cause you don't know where ya came from so quite yer moanin'."

"Alright."

"Now don't forget the plan. He's workin' late, ya go talk to him, play it nice, watch what he does an pick up them little gestures, and we'll work 'em into what you do. He's smart, he'll pick up on some bait don't worry."

"I can't help it, I do worry. I always worry."

"No more. Now go!"

Chapter Eight

*T*he New Year passed without any further sightings but Stefan was still worried about Em, she had put on a brave face but he knew that she was anxious. Stefan considered the photo on the screen, he had been looking at the same photo for the last twenty minutes and could not remember what he was looking for.

Oh yes, that tiny flaw, the mole that had to disappear. Why hadn't he seen it? He knew why — because all he had done for the last two hours was brood about Em. This unrequited love was for the birds and smaller men.

Sometimes it was all he could do to keep himself from scooping her up and taking her into the bedroom and ... well, never mind the rest. But she was just so stunning, vulnerable, irresistible, and last night was no exception she looked like the image of an angel.

It wasn't as if Stefan had never seen a beautiful woman. Known for his easy-going temperament, he was always in demand by the models and because of the quality of his photos, he was always in demand by the management.

Stefan rubbed his eyes and headed for the fridge. Pulling out a beer, he popped the top off the bottle and headed for a seat by the window to watch the people walk by, dammit, Em was rubbing off.

Reflecting on the Christmas evening he wondered who this guy that looked so much like Peter was and exactly what did he want? Not waiting any longer, Stefan pulled out his mobile phone - time for action.

It took about fifteen minutes to finish the call to his friend Bert who had been a police constable and still had friends in all the right places. He would check this guy out just as soon as Stefan had a name, and Stefan knew exactly how he was going to get it.

"Do you have everything Sarah?"

"Think so, and if I don't, I'm going to buy it."

Em hugged Sarah. "Have a swim in the ocean for me. And don't spend too much!"

Em knew full well that it was falling on deaf ears as Sarah considered it her personal goal in life to keep the local economy of La Jolla California afloat with her spending habits. As much money as Sarah made, she managed to keep her accountants busy with expenditures, investments and of course the donations to all her favourite charities on both sides of the ocean.

Sarah hugged Em and turned to finish the last of the tea and once again check her watch.

"I wish I had time for another, as a matter of fact, I wish I wasn't going. You know Em, I can postpone this trip, and work on the series later in the year."

"Oh no, you won't! Alisa and Grayson will have your hide. You promised them the winter ocean series and you can't go back on your word."

Em stood up from the kitchen table. "And don't worry about me," she said, reading Sarah's mind. "I'm fine. Really. And Roger called back with feedback on my new book, so I'll be busy."

Sarah pulled on her fur jacket then turned back to Em, her face serious. "Just promise me that if anything and I mean *anything*, bothers you that you'll call me right away? And if you think that you can hide anything don't even try. I have my sources," she said winking.

Em rolled her eyes. "What is it with you and Stefan? A conspiracy? I tried to fix you both up and now you repay me with conversations behind my back?"

Sarah tried not to look smug and failed. "I just don't know what's going on with this Peter look-a-like situation and if I had my way I'd stay and find out. I mean although Peter was a distant cousin of mine, I never really knew him I couldn't believe we were related. Seemed like a spooky six degrees of separation thing." Sarah was interrupted by Em turning her toward the door and pushing.

"Go with my blessing and I'll see you in a few weeks. Are you coming back here or staying in London?"

"You are a subtle as a sledgehammer, no I'm not going to London to see Jeff. Yes, I know he's nice, he's rich, he's a lawyer, he's gorgeous but he's not for me and neither is Stefan. So, I promise to find my own man," said Sarah, holding up her right hand.

"As if you have trouble," Em smiled, thinking of the trail that usually followed the petite Sarah around. It was like watching a parade with the various shapes and sizes of men that fell for Sarah, but none usually stuck. They couldn't survive the energy that emanated from and surrounded her like a forcefield.

The doorbell rang and Sarah flitted to the door where Stefan stood with both hands outstretched.

"Do we need six Sherpas or will I do?" he asked.

Sarah pulled two cases for Stefan to carry and clutched her carry-on that contained paperwork, makeup and her sketches. The very essence of Sarah was in that bag.

Sarah flew back to Em for a second hug, and without another word was out the door.

Stefan glanced over his shoulder, "I'll be back in about an hour. How about tea and a cake?"

Em nodded, the smile not quite reaching her cobalt eyes.

"I'll be working so just come in." With that, she shut the door then headed to the lounge, the front window and her intersection.

Mrs. McLean was just taking Snowball out for a walk, using the same gentle pull on the leash to get her to follow, the bright pink collar and leash stark against the white fur of the Himalayan cat.

Em watched and waved as Sarah got into the car and Stefan loaded the trunk, punched down the lid and then headed for the driver side.

Em's eyes wandered to her intersection to see the other lives going by, Mrs. McLean had waved and disappeared around the corner, and the morning traffic was just starting to thin out. School had not yet started so it wasn't a parade of uniforms, instead, it was pageant of the winter fashion season. The new clothes from Christmas and New Year's displayed like models on a Parisian catwalk, with brunettes, redheads, and blondes, all with long straight hair that was in-fashion at the moment. So unlike the curly dark hair that Peter had worn right to the to nape of his neck, just like...

And then she saw him. Peter's Doppelgänger. Double. Twin. Even at the distance from the third floor, Em recognised the same turn of the head. Clutching at the curtains she watched as he walked to the corner away from her then turned looking directly up at the window, right at her window, right at her, and she melted against the wall, fading into the folds of the drapes, closing her eyes while repeating the words, "It's not you, it's not you," until she felt her heartbeat begin to slow. Looking down she unclenched her hands leaving behind long wrinkles on the curtain.

Fighting the nausea she turned again looking down into the street and the fading image of Stefan's car, the corner of the intersection, the people walking home or to work or to the shop, her eyes searching for the familiar sight that wasn't there.

Did I imagine it? Em asked herself. I'm not imaging him because Tommy saw him and Sarah. Why is this happening to me? Is this part of—

She could not finish the thought. It was enough knowing that her days were safely spent inside, she knew if she stayed inside she could not be hurt by the outside world, at least it had been that way for the last three years and now this mysterious stranger was threatening her quiet safe life, even her sanity. Yet she knew she was not ready to think about why just yet.

She looked up at the clouds building up in the January sky, so formidable yet so familiar. Soon it would snow and for a time the world would be a pristine white, before becoming a washed-out dirty grey. She stood and remembered her first visit to Scotland, more specifically Glasgow. Peter was so excited, they visited the museums, tiny pubs, parks, and especially Ashton Lane, a small cobblestone street near Byres Road. He told her the story of how Sir Arthur Conan Doyle helped to free an innocent man from prison in real life, it was a particularly scary story as the original murder had been committed only a few streets away from Peter's flat. Em stood for a while feeling confused that the memories which used to cause her pain were becoming just a part of her history. Shrugging the feeling away she turned from the window and approached her computer with a new found resolution.

Soon afterward Stefan called to say he would be delayed getting back, so they agreed to lunch, and just a few hours later, both were settled in the front lounge with the remnants of a lunch of tomato soup, morning rolls with a variety of fillings, scones, cream jam, wine and now sipping an expresso Stefan broached the subject he knew he had to but dreaded doing

"So Em... we've known each other a while..." he began.

"Two years, eleven months, one week and three days," replied Em.

"I'm glad to hear that you're keeping count."

"Silly boy, I always remember the day I moved here, and then you showed up a few weeks later returning from one of your photographic expeditions."

"You certainly brightened up the neighbourhood."

Em smiled. "Flattery will get you absolutely nowhere. Why don't you find a nice girl to spend it on?"

"I do," Stefan said and waved his hand before Em could argue.

"What about you and a nice man? What about Peter? What was he like?"

The silence stretched for a moment as Em sipped the strong coffee, thinking about the man she loved and adored so much. As she had reflected earlier it didn't cause the physical pain anymore. When he first died, she sometimes wondered how she could go on with the huge black hole in the middle of her chest where her heart had been, and then after losing— No, she wasn't going to think about that now.

"Em?"

Breaking away from her thoughts, Em put down the cup, rose and went to the window.

"Don't you ever wonder about their lives, Stefan? Who they go home to? Are they happy? Sad? Rich, or poor? Do they have a big family or are they alone?"

Em felt rather than heard Stefan behind her, and as she leaned back into the comfort of his arms, she knew she was strong enough for the story. With one last look out the window, she turned to Stefan and looked up. Her head barely touched his chin, and as he returned her gaze she noticed that his eyes, usually a light blue, were darker, like the ocean on a stormy day.

"Peter was perfect." She felt Stefan stand just a little straighter and continued, "more coffee first."

The ritual of coffee making soothed the shaky feeling. Was it just Peter? Or was it the way she had felt in Stefan's arms for a moment? The comfort, the peace, almost contentment, she had rarely ever felt that before, even with Peter. With him, it was fun and passion and knowing each other so well. He wasn't perfect as she had said, he was just perfect for her. He knew her moods and if she were a little sad, he could make her laugh at the silliest stories just by how he told them.

"You're awfully quiet," Stefan observed.

"I know. I'm just trying to sort out ... telling you about Peter."

Coffee made and in large mugs, they returned to the comfort of the front lounge and settled onto the sofa, Em with her legs up under her.

"Did you know he was a brilliant scientist?"

"Yes," Stefan nodded. That's how you met right? He went to California?

"Yes," answered Em smiling at the memory of their first meeting.

"He was brilliant. It was because of his innovative breakthrough in the nuclear power industry that first brought him to California. It was a five-day conference in San Diego and I went because I have always been fascinated with anything to do with the nuclear research."

Em stopped when she saw Stefan's face wreathed in smiles. "Do you want to hear the story or not?" she threatened. "I know I'm not a scientist or engineer, but I do have a weakness."

"Go on, go on, I can take it," Stefan said as he pulled her feet over to rest on his lap and she ended up facing him.

"Alright," Em hesitated for just a moment before continuing, "I met Peter there. The lecture hall was packed, I had arrived early and of course, was sitting up front. Alisa was there too, but for a different reason."

"Of course," Stefan smiled again.

"Anyway, he was giving his lecture and, don't ask me how, but his eyeglasses, which he was holding in his hands as he spoke took flight ended up in my lap."

"He probably threw them there. I know I would have."

"Stefan!"

"Okay, okay please go on."

Em was silent for a moment, not because she was upset - she was not - she was actually feeling good about being able to share memories of Peter with someone she cared for.

Stefan closed his lips and made the locking sign with his fingers and threw the key to Em, which made her laugh. She caught the imaginary key and tucked it into the pocket of her jeans.

Settling down she began the story again.

"I went up to return his glasses and he pulled me onto the lecture area and proceeded to use me for the next 10 minutes as a part of his talk. Once he was finished, he introduced me to his colleagues and said that the least he could do was buy me lunch in recompense for using me as a live part of his lecture. And then he never left," Em paused to sip her coffee and with a far-away look in her eyes continued, "he was supposed to be there for about a week as he was on research leave and was originally headed for Australia with a few lectures along the way. He decided to stay in San Diego and work on the project from there. And of course, when the University heard that the brilliant Peter Lawson was staying they immediately offered him the facilities if he would use some of their researchers on his new project."

Em frowned as her memory jumped to the day he died. "He wasn't supposed to be there. He wasn't...we were packing that day and —" Em's voice caught at the pain of the memory.

"He went into the lab and it exploded." Silent tears rolled down her face

Stefan's voice was gentle and quiet. "Where were you when it happened?"

Em looked at Stefan though the cloud of tears. "I don't know. I remember him leaving and I remember him kissing me goodbye and I remember him waving from the car, and then I don't remember anything else until I woke up in the hospital."

Stefan's hand balled into itself as he saw the pain and sadness on Em's face.

She looked at Stefan. "I've never been able to remember that afternoon, the day my husband died... And the day I lost our child."

Chapter Nine

*S*arah stretched her arms to reach the top of the chaise lounge and wiggled her toes. It was her first day off in three weeks, although she didn't necessarily consider painting to be work. It was her passion from that first day when she crawled into the hall closet, found the watercolours and proceeded to paint the bathroom, and she had not stopped painting since then. Her sketches won awards in primary school and by the time she went to university she was recognised for her unique talent and was a well-paid artist.

She had only gone to University to please her mother who insisted that she get a degree so she could be independent and support herself. It never failed to amaze Sarah that her mother could never quite come to terms with the money she made from her paintings. Her mother had always supported it as a hobby, and while Anne loved her daughter and her paintings, Anne always thought of it as just a hobby, not a profession.

Grayson and Alisa had been patrons of Sarah's work for almost a decade and whenever they had a special request she would generally interrupt her schedule to accommodate them, and it didn't hurt that they had one of the most expensive and luxurious homes in La Jolla, the ocean community just north of San Diego and would insist that she stay there while working.

The mansion sat on top of a craggy bluff, floor to ceiling windows in every room faced the ocean providing stunning views. Marble floors, high arched ceilings and large rooms gave a feeling of being part of the surrounding nature rather than a house sitting on it.

"Sarah, lunch will be in about an hour. Would you like red or white wine as an apéritif?"

Grayson stood blocking the sun, so Sarah didn't have to squint up at him. Tall with black hair, the most striking feature of Grayson's Apache heritage was his cheekbones. Sarah once informed Alisa that if she left Grayson she would be right in there to bring comfort. Alisa had laughed as she said, "Go for it - but I warn you as soon as the war paint goes on…."

"White please," Sarah requested.

"Excellent choice madam," Grayson said, playing the waiter. "I am happy to offer you Château Carbonnieux Blanc please do note beautiful pale yellow with slight green hues, with notes of grapefruit and aromas of apricot."

Sarah burst into giggles at the serious expression on Grayson's face as he poured a small sample for her to taste, and then he winked which caused another fit of laughter.

"Grayson, I have an idea. Why don't you and Alisa just adopt me, and I can live out the rest of my life in this palace you call home?"

Grayson wagged his finger, "Oh no, I have enough of a time trying to please one woman."

"After twenty years of marriage if you don't know how to please me," Alisa's wheelchair had silently glided onto the patio.

At forty, Alisa was usually mistaken for twenty-five, and the stunning long blonde hair and green-eyed beauty that had made her a top model for fifteen years had not diminished. Her perfect features had only softened and refined in the last ten years. The only reminder of her car accident five years ago was the motorised wheelchair she used, it was only after too many operations that Alisa decided she did not want to be a guinea pig for every new procedure and so lived a full and eventful life on two or four wheels.

Alisa continued, "that was Em on the phone. She said for you to call her when you have a minute, and if you're wondering why she didn't call you on your mobile it was because she thought you might be working and didn't want to disturb you. She said to call after lunch for a catch-up."

Sarah twisted on the lounge. "How did she sound? Was she okay? I mean should I call her now?"

"No, no, I think after lunch is fine, and she sounded good, quite happy in fact. I wondered if she's been out at all?" Alisa mused.

"I wish but no, she won't even go see that psychiatrist you found for her in Glasgow. She is intent on staying in that flat, which she designed exactly as Peter had wanted it's a safety net for her and so she hasn't been out since. Do you believe it's been three years?"

"Why won't she see the doctor?" Grayson asked, returning with the three wine glasses and waving away Mary, who supervised the household staff and seemed to appear by magic when anything was needed.

"She's done quite a bit of research into Agoraphobia and recognises the symptoms but swears that she is quite happy to live her life there in the flat, the one she's dedicated to Peter. Did I tell you about the doppelgänger?"

"What!?" exclaimed Grayson and Alisa together.

"Well, there is this man who looks exactly like Peter and he's been seen a couple of times and actually confronted young Tommy. He asked Tommy about the "pretty lady with the curly hair", it freaked her right out. I wonder if he's been around again?"

Sarah's question hung in the air unanswered as lunch was served. Smoked salmon, capers, cream cheese, a platter of mixed sandwiches, grapes, kiwi fruit, oranges and a tower of chocolate brownies.

Sarah groaned, "Are you sure you guys don't want to adopt me?"

"So, how's California life?" Em asked.

Sarah sighed. "I think I've died and gone to decadent heaven. You would not believe the food and the wine and the chocolate."

"Have you done any work?"

"Yes, I have! As a matter of fact, the series of sketches is complete two paintings are done and I am going to stay on for just a couple of weeks more and then head back home, to Scotland." Sarah specified which home as she had four others, Monterey, London, Paris, and one on the tiny Greek island of Kefalonia. Keeping track could be a challenge.

"While you're still there would you mind doing me a favour?"

"Sure hun - name it."

"Well, it has to do with Peter's doppelgänger."

"What!"

"Hold on oh excitable one. First, you are not going to believe this, just after you left, Stefan asked about Peter, after all the year's I've known him." Em briefly related the conversation then continued, "and just about a week later Derek - that's the name of Peter's look-a-like - showed up at the door. I have to admit I about fell over, I've seen him on the street and Tommy's watched out for him, but he hasn't been around lately, then all of a sudden he was there. Stefan has been home lately and I called him and he came over for support."

Em took a breath.

"And…" prompted Sarah.

"Well, this Derek claims to be Peter's brother, and that they were separated at birth. Of all the ridiculous, idiotic, insane ideas that I've heard! I thought this just happens in movies, bad American movies at that. The long lost brother showing up and wanting to worm his way into the family and who knows what? Well, I do know what, it's always about money."

"Oh my gosh, I do not believe this!"

"Wait, Sarah, I'm not done. He said that he saw Peter before he died and that Peter was going to introduce us and bring him into the family."

"Hold on, just a minute, how is it I've never heard of this? I mean I was Peter's cousin, and I know the family. I know that Peter's mom died at childbirth, but the births would have been recorded."

"Not necessarily," Em said. "Remember that Elizabeth gave birth to Peter while they were in Italy visiting her family and that Stewart wasn't even there."

"Yes, that's true. But why would they hide it? And what the devil does he want?"

"I'll tell you all about when you get back, and yes, you'll just have to wait. I've got to sort this out, so I'm going to write it all out and sort it chronologically."

"What can I do to help?"

Em explained what she wanted.

Sarah clicked the phone off turned to head back to the patio and jumped.

"Alisa!"

"Sorry, Sarah! I wasn't eavesdropping, honest."

"No worries, I just hadn't heard you come in is all."

"I know," she smiled. "Gray had this new wheelchair designed and it's so quiet - I sneak up on him all the time now. More importantly, how is Em?"

"Surprisingly good considering what's going on. I wonder if Stefan has got something do with that?" Sarah was silent for a moment. "I need to check out a few things at the University. Would you mind if I borrowed one of your cars?"

"No problem. Which one?" asked Alisa. "Actually, would you mind if I come along? I've got a new SUV."

"Of course not, I think that's a great idea."

"As a matter of fact, I'll just call the chancellor and find out who would be best suited for us to speak to."

Sarah smiled and bent to hug Alisa. "You are absolutely fabulous!"

Alisa returned the hug then admonished Sarah, "In the meantime let's have another glass of that lovely white while you fill me in on all the details."

Chapter Ten

*T*he next morning Sarah and Alisa drove from the palatial retreat to the University of California. They followed the coastal route south to San Diego, a long winding road that follows the natural line of the coast with the Pacific Ocean on their right.

Driving onto the grounds, Sarah pulled up next to the security booth.

"Hi Fred, how are you today?"

"Fine, Mrs. Drew, how are you doing, and Mr. Drew, is he okay too?" Fred raised his stark white eyebrows which resembled two albino caterpillars sitting on top of pale grey eyes.

"He's managing to stay out of trouble, just barely," Alisa smiled. "We're here to see Simon Hawthorne."

"Yes, Mrs. Drew you just head over to your usual parking place."

A brief wave and the SUV glided the short distance to the parking area.

Video cameras captured every person entering the University grounds, as was standard policy since the explosion three years ago, the explosion which had killed Peter and brought the nuclear research to a grinding halt for several months while the investigation went on. Sarah had rarely visited since then, usually due to her duties as one of the largest benefactors to the university.

Alisa stopped at the specific disabled parking spot closest to the administration office, which was allocated to her.

"Sometimes it pays off," Alisa said.

"What does?"

"Disabled parking. I never have to walk far, I mean, *go* far."
Alisa turned toward Sarah smiling.

Sarah laughed. "I don't know how you do it, Alisa. You are
always so happy, and I know it was horrible after the accident."

"Yes, it was. But I had Gray and he was phenomenal, as was
Em. He still is, he's always trying to make every bit of life easier
for me, designing new gadgets and streamlining the existing
ones. At least the operations have stopped. We tried every new
procedure and I just got tired of it. I mean, we have a full life,"
Alisa said, glancing sideways at Sarah. "A very full life."

Sarah caught her meaning and actually blushed, which was
not common for her and hurriedly said. "Well we'd better head
in to see this guy. And am I glad you made the call, it sounded as
if he didn't want to talk to me at all."

"Well, Sarah, as much money as we've given to this university
I thought it might pave the way a little. Besides, I'd do anything
to get a little excitement, and I always thought that there was
something suspicious about the explosion. I mean Peter was
always so cautious with materials, and the investigation just
glossed over things a little too neatly, and Simon is still head of
the research department here."

"I just hope that he will open up."

Alisa pressed a button on the car's consul and her chair
swivelled and lowered to the ground. She pressed another and
the back passenger door of the custom BMW slid back. One
more button and the motorised wheelchair slid quietly to the
ground next to where Alisa sat. She moved deftly from the seat to
the chair, and the passenger seat automatically slid up and back
into the car.

Sarah watched. "Way cool!"

"Oh yes, most everything in my life is as easy as the push of a
button. Gray has even set all the doors in the house on a remote
and a sensor, so when my wheelchair goes near a door it opens
automatically. It's quite fun, I can run around the house opening

all the doors, drives Mary nuts. See, I do have a wicked part to my nature!"

"Wicked sense of humour you mean."

A few minutes later they were ushered into the office of the Director of Research for the university, Simon Hawthorne.

"Hello, Mrs. Drew and Miss Livingstone."

"Hello Simon — and please call me Alisa, we've known each other too long for this formality," Alisa smiled and extended her slim long-fingered hand. It was promptly pumped up and down with the chubby fingers of the Director of Research.

"So we have," Simon agreed.

Sarah extended her hand, "And please call me Sarah."

"And I'm Simon. May I offer you coffee? Tea? A soda?"

"No, thank you, Simon, we just need a few minutes of your time." Alisa turned toward Sarah. "Sarah just has a few questions about the time when Peter Lawson worked here."

Simon clasped his hands and rubbed the palms back and forth. "Well, you know that the information from the accident is confidential and not to be released to the public, as it's still an on-going investigation."

Alisa raised her eyebrows. "Now Simon that was three years ago. What could you still be investigating after all this time?"

Simon's large lips pursed, relaxed and pursed again making him look like a large goldfish, clearly trying to assess how much information he could give to satisfy his visitors_without really giving away any information.

"Simon," Alisa's tone deepened, she paused looking him directly in the eyes and said, "you know, Gray and I have been speaking about that new lab you would like to open. Just the other night we thought that a Casino Charity night would be a good idea for a way to raise the money for the lab and the equipment. What do you think?"

Simon's eyes widened and his chubby fingers did a quick tap dance on the desktop. Reaching a decision, he called in his secretary. "Would you please get me the Lawson file?"

"Yes sir," she said and disappeared, returning a few minutes later with a medium-sized paper box.

"All the documents are in here, Mr Hawthorne."

Sarah viewed the box with dismay - she hated paperwork and refused to do it. She had thought that they would just ask a few questions, make a few notes and be done. She thought, *this looks horrendous.*

"Thank you, Simon," Alisa said. "We promise to return them later this afternoon."

Simon's white face turned whiter. "Well, uh, I don't think—"

"Oh Simon, don't worry. We will take excellent care of them and Mary will bring the entire file back later today."

"I really don't know…" He considered briefly, then decided. "well Alisa, since *it is* you."

He hesitated for another moment. If he was going to release this file he wanted to ensure funds for the lab would come in, his reputation for raising money was legendary.

"Did you have an idea of a night for the charity Mrs. Drew - ah ah Alisa?"

Alisa's smile was genuine but not as warm, "Well I think that a Springtime Casino night will bring in quite a bit. I have some friends who are out of the country at the moment, but they'll be returning in a few weeks and then I'll arrange it. What if we hold it at the University Centre? I'll order an architect's rendition, and if you have an idea of the equipment then we can prepare a list, and…" She stopped short, looking apologetically at Sarah.

"Anyway Simon, I'll be in touch next week to coordinate. By the way, Simon, do you remember anything particularly unusual around the time before the explosion? Where there any uncommon groups or unusual persons hanging around Peter's lab in the days before the tragedy?"

Simon scratched the front of his balding head considering. "That was, what, three years ago winter time? No, not really, but I was Director of Research then and wasn't involved so much with every department. We didn't have the video set up until afterwards, but…"

Simon trailed off and called once again for his secretary.

"Moira, do you remember anything in particular before the… the event of three years ago?" Simon hated the word explosion.

Moira considered her words. "Well, sir the documents in the box are quite detailed. But now that you mention it there was something a bit peculiar."

All three leaned forward in unison.

"Professor Lawson was seen going into his lab in the early afternoon, and then about ten minutes later someone saw him in the guest parking lot."

Simon gave her a questioning look and Moira continued. "Well, the guest parking lot is at the opposite end of the campus, about 25 minutes from his lab. There isn't any way he could've gotten from his lab to the guest parking lot in that time. Also, why would he park there when he had driven in and parked in his allocated space? It was Sammy the janitor who saw him in the lot and waved at him, but Professor Lawson just continued walking. Sammy thought it was unusual because he looked right at Sammy and didn't even seem to recognise him." Moira continued, "I think that's the only item not in the notes and that's only because Sammy didn't think of it at the time, we were just talking about it at the dedication, you know, when they rebuilt the lab."

Sarah looked at Alisa and slightly shook her head.

"Thank you, Moira," Alisa said.

Moira nodded silently and looked at Simon. "Anything else Mr Hawthorne?"

"No Moira. Oh yes, would you please let Mr Todd know I'll be there in about 10 minutes?"

Thanks expressed and box in hand, Sarah and Alisa headed back to her vehicle.

An hour later Sarah, Alisa and Gray sat in the living room each enjoying a glass of wine, with the box in the safe hands of Mary who was going to copy every scrap of paper before returning the box and its contents to the University.

Sarah filled Alisa and Gray in on the Peter / Derek story, and they considered that this was the proof that Derek had visited Peter, including the fact that it was so close to the time of the explosion.

"Oh, by the way, Gray, I had to promise a casino charity event to raise money for a new lab for the university."

"I hope Simon appreciates how much you do for that university," commented Gray.

"Well, it got us the box. Now we just need to dig through it."

Sarah hid behind the glass of wine, dreading the idea of all those bits of paper and trying to piece them together.

Alisa saw Sarah's expression and giggled. "Heavens Sarah you should see your face. It looks like you're going to an exam and you don't know the subject."

"Just prepare the plasters," Sarah said. "I get paper cuts just looking at those things."

"Well, as soon as Mary's done copying, we can go through it together."

Sarah went over and hugged Alisa. "Thank you. I don't know what I would have done without you. Simon would not have given me the time of day."

"No problem, it really is my pleasure, now should you call Em and let her know about Derek being spotted?"

"Not yet Alisa. Let's wait till we go through the box and see if we have anything else to report."

Chapter Eleven

"Tommy it's your move."

In the weeks since the Christmas party, Em had accepted Tommy as her chess partner, and in a short time, he was proving to be a challenging and interesting player. The schedule was once a week, on the Saturday after he completed the morning delivery, he would stay, they would have tea and start a game.

"Sorry Mrs. er… Em." Tommy blinked his blue eyes and stared at the board. He had also been instructed that since he was old enough to play chess with her, he was old enough to call her Em. It had taken a few weeks, but he was settling into both.

"What is it? Are you worried about maths again?"

"No, I… it's just, I made a promise and I don't think I should keep it, and I just don't know what to do."

Em looked at the troubled freckled face. "When you make a promise to someone it is important to keep your word."

"But what if you didn't want to make the promise, but they told you that something bad would happen if you broke your promise?" Tommy asked as his brow furrowed in worry.

"Well, I don't think that anyone should be forced to make a promise. A promise is your word of honour and should be given freely, otherwise… it is a problem."

"Em, I don't know what to do."

"Okay. Is it boy stuff or girl stuff?"

"It involves a girl."

"Then why don't you talk to Stefan? He's good at girl stuff and he may be able to help you find a way to keep your promise without hurting anyone."

Tommy brightened. "Great idea! He's really nice."

Stefan had started coming round for tea in the mornings and was often there when Tommy stopped by and they would talk about football, definitely boy stuff.

"Can I go now Em?" Tommy asked.

"Of course. We'll leave the game set up and continue it the next time. How about that?"

"Sure!" Tommy leapt off the chair and zipped out of the door definitely on a mission.

Em's mobile vibrated, and she smiled at the picture that popped into view as she answered.

"Em?"

"Hi, Sarah. How goes it?"

"Well I think we've found something, but I'm not sure."

"Okay, what have you found? And when and how?" Em asked eagerly.

Sarah related the events and Alisa's help and the efficient Mary and Moira.

"So, it sounds as if Derek did go to see Peter."

"Yep, and he was there the day of the explosion. But did he see Peter beforehand or was he pre-empted or what? Anyway, that's not all. We found a set of keys."

"And?" Em prompted

"Well, it's got what looks like house keys, a safety deposit key and a skeleton key. Now they don't use skeleton keys here in California, so do you know what it might be for? The flat or anything else?"

Em considered for a moment a memory that tickled her, but she couldn't put her finger on it.

"Not sure Sarah. I'll tell you what, bring it home with you and we'll check around. I have a funny feeling, but I just can't

51

remember." She considered it a moment longer. "Nope, it's not coming to me right now. Anything else?"

"Well Em, I think I'm going to leave a little early. I talked to Grey and Alisa and they're happy with how the series is progressing and I promised to return in about a month. That will work best as I can get some more sketches when the weather is closer to spring."

"Sounds great," Em said and laughing added. "Would you like me to pick you up at the airport?"

"What!?"

"Just kidding. Although I wish I wasn't."

"And how is your work going?"

"Quiet. My intersection has been quieter than usual. Don't they know that they form an integral part of my life and it's just not the same without them?"

"Probably not. And if you got out a little…"

"Don't start dear one. I can joke about it but… let's just let it go. I'm sorry I brought it up."

"I'm not! Eventually, it will have to change, and you can make it work in your own good time. A walk down the street, going out to the cinema, dinner or dancing. Remember the fun we used to have going out on the town?"

Em sighed. "I remember, and I miss it. It's just I don't have to worry about what might happen. If I'm home I can handle any situation, but out there, it's dangerous, it's deadly, and I don't want to be a part of it. At least not right now."

"Enough said. I'll be home in a few days. If there are any changes or updates just give me a call."

"Of course and give my love to Alisa and Gray."

As the connection clicked off Em realized just what the key was for. Oh well, it had waited three years, it could wait another few days.

❧

"So have you talked to her yet?"

"No, not yet."

"And will you put out that cigarette, it's disgusting."

"Converts are always the worst." He observed as he stubbed out the cigarette, grinding it into the ashtray.

"Well, I wish you'd hurry up. What are you waiting for? She's never left that flat. What is it with her anyway? You'd think she was an old woman afraid to leave the house!"

Derek sat back in the spindly chair viewing the cracked linoleum on the floor. *God this place makes me sick*, he thought. *Why do I wait?* He had to admit just watching her from the street he wanted to talk to her, to hear the voice that matched that beautiful face. It was so expressive when she watched out the window, she never seemed to tire of the people passing and he knew he never tired of watching her. She would shake her head at something and the blonde curls would bounce and frame that heart-shaped pale skinned beauty.

Will I be able to go through with it? He wondered and then realised that he did not know, but whatever happened he was going to meet her, and, well, whatever happened he would deal with it.

"You'd better do something soon. That red-headed kid might say something to someone eventually, and then where will we be?"

"Yeah, yeah, quit nagging you're getting on my nerves." He slammed the drink on the table, spilling the whiskey over the edge. As he licked his fingers, he considered his options and made a decision.

cₛ№

Sarah clicked off the phone with Em and wondered what else to do before she left. The paperwork in the box had not proved to be very insightful.

Peter's research into safe options for nuclear waste disposal was controversial and considered as one possibility for the explosion that had killed him, but there wasn't any direct evidence that anyone had that as a motive. As her only cousin, they had been as close as they could be in the circumstances.

Chapter Twelve

*J*ames Armistead was at least a head shorter than Stefan, but that never made a difference when he was angry.

"What the hell do you think you're doing?!"

Stefan had the grace to look ashamed but held his ground.

"I know it wasn't the smartest thing to do, but I'd had enough. When Tommy came to me and told me what this Derek jerk was up to, I just lost it —a bit."

"A bit! A bit!?"

"Well, if he would've…"

He was interrupted by James, once again heated voice. "You went out onto the street in broad daylight and hit a guy for absolutely no reason! No reason! Other than the fact he has got designs on your girl."

"She's not my girl." Stefan's voice was low and tinged with sadness.

"That's even worse! Do you want this going on your record? Do you want to jeopardise this operation?"

"Enough James. I said I'm sorry."

"I didn't hear it."

"Well, I thought it. Anyway, what did you find out?"

"How could you do that? And now you have the unmitigated gall to expect me to use company resources to investigate this nobody?"

"Yes, " Stefan answered.

James was silent for a moment. In all the years he had known Stefan he had never known him to make such a huge mistake involving a possible crime, and he hated it. Stefan ran his own investigations in his own time, and no one was ever the wiser. James didn't know if it was the fact that Stefan looked like an easygoing photographer, or that he could hypnotise the world, but whatever it was, it worked. And now, for the first time, Stefan had drawn attention to himself by punching some idiot on the street, in front of witnesses.

James ran his fingers over his head, wishing he had hair he could tear out. It seemed like such a small incident, but the last thing he needed was the police starting an investigation on Stefan.

"It's not a big deal James, really."

"It had better not be Stefan, we've got too much riding on this. Too many years have gone into this to come so close for you to screw it up at the last minute, and if I thought, even for a minute that you would cause this operation to go south! We have never come so close to arresting this sorry piece of work, he has hidden behind so many…"

"James I won't, I would never endanger a case, you of all people know that!" Stefan stopped and regarded his boss before continuing, "You've talked to this guy, right? So he's got a bloody nose. I'll go make nice with him. Honest!"

James shook his head. "You are so lucky that you're my best agent because if you weren't you'd be—"

"I'd be what?" Stefan interrupted. "Fired? You can't do that. Remember James, technically I don't work for you, I'm doing you a really big favour, and it's only because I'm good and well placed that you're even using me. So don't try to intimidate me, that's just laughable."

James got up from behind the desk and opened the door resigned to the fact that he would never change Stefan when he believed he was right.

"Just go talk to the guy and do make nice okay? This operation will be done in a few weeks and then you can do whatever, but until that time…"

"I know, I know, stay out of trouble," Stefan sighed. He rarely lost his temper, and it all came down to protecting Em. No woman had ever caused him so much grief, at least one that he hadn't slept with, hadn't even had a proper date with. Well, that was only because she never left the house. *Shit!*, he jammed his hands in his pockets and walked out the door determined to find out from this Derek what the hell he was up to, all without blowing an operation he had devoted two years of his life to.

Em sat on the sofa in the lounge looking at the TV without seeing or hearing a word. What could Stefan have been thinking? What had possessed him to punch Derek? She admitted to herself she was a bit shaken when she saw Derek on the street corner this afternoon. It was like seeing Peter reincarnated, and then to see her friend, her dear friend, go out and - it didn't bear thinking about.

The doorbell rang, interrupting the muddle of thoughts.

"Hi Em. Can I come in?"

"Of course Tommy, although I don't know if it's a good time to continue the chess game."

"It's okay. I just wanted to talk to you anyway."

Em looked at her young red-headed friend, hands pushed so hard into his pockets that the seams threatened to split, and she immediately wanted to give him a hug.

"Come into the lounge and we can have a hot chocolate, how about that?"

"Yes please." he face brightening as he blushed.

A few minutes later Em faced Tommy.

"I'm so sorry about what happened, I didn't know it would make him so angry and I didn't know what to do and I couldn't tell you 'cause I said I wouldn't, and I know it's important to keep your word and I wanted to do that and I didn't want to tell my Dad and now it's—" Tommy looked up as Em put up her hand.

"Tommy..." she said, her voice quiet and reassuring. "I'm not sure what you want to say, but why don't you start at the beginning. Slowly please."

Tommy took a sip of the hot chocolate and with a small brown moustache started his story.

"Well, remember when we were playing chess the other day?" He waited for confirmation.

"Yes, I do," Em assured him.

"Well, I went to talk to Stefan like you suggested and I think I made him mad, and I don't want him to be mad at me."

"Why should he be mad at you?"

" 'Cause he went out and hit that guy and it was on account of me."

"What?"

"Well, Derek, the guy who looks like the man in your pictures..."

"Yes, like Peter, my husband..."

"Yes. Well, he talked to me about a week ago and asked me to keep it a secret. He said that he wanted to surprise you and that it would make you happy, but if I told you then you would be unhappy."

"Told me what Tommy?"

"Well, that's the problem. He made me promise and I don't want to break it, but when I told Stefan he got mad and then when he saw him today he hit him, and now I don't know what to do." Tommy's face fell once again before he took another sip of the hot chocolate.

"Tommy, are you telling me that you told the secret to Stefan and he then went out and hit Derek? And now you are saying you can't tell me because you promised not to tell me?"

"Yes."

"Well don't you worry. I'll get Stefan to tell me and then you won't have broken your promise? Okay?"

Tommy looked even more miserable. "Well, except Stefan promised to keep the secret too."

Em rolled her eyes. The world had decidedly gone mad, Tommy driving her to distraction about his promise and now Stefan had made a promise. Well too bad! Someone was going to break their word today and she knew just who it was going to be.

"Stefan, have you completely gone off the rails?" While Em's tone sounded peeved, it was mitigated by the red wine she poured into his glass.

Tommy was gone and Stefan had arrived home about ten minutes later, after a vigilant afternoon.

Stefan held the glass to his nose. "You do have the best taste in wine," he observed while ignoring Em's question.

Em sat on the opposite sofa, and Stefan patted the seat next to him.

"No," she replied, emphatically shaking her head, making her blond curls bounce from side to side. "I want an answer."

"No, you don't. You don't what to hear what that misfit is trying to sell. That scum Derek is—"

"Stefan, I want to know what's going on," she interrupted.

Stefan surveyed her and saw the familiar determination and relented. "He says he's your husband."

Em was nonplussed. She took a sip of wine and wondered why she wasn't shaking, why she wasn't furious, shocked, devastated. Why did she feel nothing?

Stefan watched her closely for a reaction

Finally, after a few minutes, she said, "I want to meet him."

"What!?"

"I want to know why he thinks he can come here and try to see me and claim to be Peter. What is he thinking?"

"To move into your life."

"Will you go and speak to him?"

"Well…"

"Well, what Stefan? I thought you'd be…" Em stopped and looked at his expression. "What have you done?"

"I kind of lost my temper and…"

"And what?"

"Gave him a bit of a punch in the face."

Em laughed. Not at what he said but at the expression on his face. He looked like a six-year-old boy who had made a big mess and now had to confess to it.

"I'm glad you think it's funny," he said, confused yet pleased by her reaction.

"Oh no, it's not funny, but you are! And now you have to do this for me. Please? You can even be here to supervise. I just don't want him wandering down the street and Sarah will be back tomorrow. Arrange for him to come for coffee tomorrow afternoon, and we'll both be ready." Em had a thought. "How would you find him anyway? I gather he's not camped outside my window."

"Don't worry. I know where he lives."

"How do you know he'll come?"

A chance to see you Em? He'll come even if he thinks it's a trap."

C380

"How did you manage it?"

"Well, I didn't get my nose almost broken for nothing. I'm meeting her tomorrow."

"How are you going to play it?"

"Just like we talked about."

"Okay, well lay off the booze for a day."

"It's all arranged. I'm just topping up tonight instead of tomorrow," Derek sniggered, the smirk ruining his handsome features. He downed his whisky and poured himself another, throwing that one back too.

"What's with you? I thought you'd be chomping at the bit for this."

Derek remembered the view, the moon lighting up the window and her silhouette, the sadness reflected as she watched the intersection below. He poured another drink, downed the glass and left the bottle on the table, walking over to the window. *How would he play it?* He didn't know. He would wait until he could see her and then...then he would decide.

CRBO

Sarah spluttered the coffee. "He said what?!"

"Stefan said he'd bring him by about three this afternoon."

"You can't possibly believe that he's Peter?"

"No, I don't, but I want to know what his game is and question him about being at the lab on the day of the explosion, and I can't do that unless I meet him. Anyway, Stefan will be here for protection. So what else did you find out in California? And how do you have the nerve to eat like you do and stay so tiny?"

Sarah smiled, licked the sugar from the doughnut off her fingers and selected another from the pile in front of her.

"Great metabolism," she said. "And you're not exactly rolling about yourself! How you do it without going out I don't know."

"Good metabolism," Em replied and helped herself to another doughnut as well.

Tommy had brought the treat himself as an offering for the trouble he thought he had caused.

"I had to let Tommy down about the chess game this afternoon with the Derek thing going on. Too bad, he's becoming a good little player."

"Great, I'm glad. Now, will you tell me what this key belongs to? I mean what does it fit into?"

"Ah, glad you asked Watson!" Em stood up, dusting her fingers, and waggled one at Sarah. "Follow me," she requested leading Sarah into the converted master closet and showing her the small door tucked behind the shoe tower in the corner.

Sarah removed the key from her pocket and gave it to Em, who fitted it into the lock of the half-sized door. The key turned and with a small gentle push broke the seal of paint around the edge as the door squeaked, groaned and finally gave way.

The room was narrow but normal height, so they both ducked under the door into the long room.

"I had forgotten about this in the plans," said Em. "Peter hadn't shown anything to be done with it, so I just left it alone."

"Of course you did," said Sarah. "You did exactly what he wanted."

Em shot a look at Sarah. It had been the only thing they had ever disagreed on. Sarah didn't understand why Em had followed Peter's plan for the flat perfectly, moved in and never left. She couldn't understand, yet she recognised how important it was to Em, up to a point. So eventually they had agreed to disagree, and not discuss it further. But sometimes it just came up.

The room was used for storage and had tall bookshelves running along the left side, chock full of books, though there was still enough room to walk past the shelving toward the back of the room. At the end was another door, which accepted the same key, and as Em turned the lock and pushed into the second room she stopped. Sarah, following closely behind, stopped just short of running into Em.

"What is it?"

Em turned. "What do you think?" she asked.

Sarah edged around Em and looked into a tiny room set up like an office, with a desk and chair below a tiny round window.

In the corner sat an old large steamer trunk and when Em opened it she gasped. "Look at all these old photos Sarah!"

Sarah turned from her examination of the desk to see the truck full of black and white photos that were yellowing with age.

"Wow, wait a minute let me see."

Sarah took the photo from Em that she had picked up from the pile. "That's our grandmother," she said. "And here is old Uncle Albert. I remember visiting them once in Italy. Gran seemed like she was four-hundred-years-old then, but here she only looks two hundred. Where was this taken?" she asked as she tapped the photo against her lip.

Em got more to the point. "If you try to figure this out about each photo we'll be here till the coming of the next Ice Age."

"Okay, okay." Sarah loved the artistry of old photos and laughing said, "Oh, I'll bet Stefan would have a good old time in here sifting through these."

"What makes you think he would know anything?" Em asked.

"Well, he is a photographer."

"Yes Sarah, but he doesn't know the people or the places. That would be like you knowing the place of a strange painting you've never seen before, just because you're a painter," Em laughed.

"I really do hate it when you bring logic into a conversation, now quit. What are we supposed to be looking for anyway?"

"I'm not sure," said Em. "A clue, but I don't know what it will be. Some insight into Derek, find out if he actually is a relation. Some insight into Peter's death. I mean I just don't know. I've always felt there was something wrong with the way he died. He went to the office at 2 p.m., but the time was really 3 p.m. because we hadn't changed the clocks forward an hour."

"Why did he go in on a Sunday again?"

"He got a call and said that he was going to meet a colleague for just half an hour. It had to do with some new research they were going to start and we were leaving the next day, so he was going to turn over the key to the lab and introduce his assistant. To be honest Sarah, it was all too fresh back then and I— " She paused. "I just wanted to be here, to be in the flat that we were to share, I wanted to feel safe again. I didn't want anything to intrude or interfere with me coming here."

Sarah was unusually quiet, letting Em say what she needed to say.

Em continued, "I know you don't agree with what I've done but it was the only way I could deal with losing Peter and the baby. First mom died when I was born and I know dad loved me, but he was gone all the time, and if it wasn't for Aunt Mary and

Uncle Bob I don't know. I remember when Aunt Mary would get mad at me for something I would just hide out in the attic, or there was this great little nook in the closet and I could read by flashlight, all by myself and it was safe. I was safe."

Em paused as a single tear edged out of her eye, and Sarah waited.

"And it only took me three years to open up about it. Not that I'm slow."

"Hey, Em please don't knock it. At least you are finally opening up, and I never knew that, about when you were little, I mean. We're all different and I know how much you loved Peter and how much he loved you, it's just, well, do you think he would want you to live your life so secluded and so…"

"I'm not secluded," Em cut her short. "I don't live on a desert island. I have company over."

"Yes, you do but you never go out, and I know you say you get enough watching people on the intersection, but that is only a small part of the whole world and you deserve the whole world. You should —" Sarah stopped. "I'm sorry Em, I know that I said I wouldn't bring it up again but you know how I feel and I know I shouldn't push my feelings onto you. I just hate to see you not living your life."

Em rolled her eyes. "I am living Sarah, but I do know what you mean. I need to get out. I have to say that I'm just worried. I don't remember what happened when Peter died, I just ended up in the hospital with you there and I had lost the baby, my life went from joy to devastation in just a few hours. I know that I need to get out, I just don't know how to get myself to do it." And with that Em turned out of the little room and said, "Come on, it's about 1 o'clock, let's go have another coffee before we meet this Derek. We can go through all this stuff tomorrow. I mean it's been here for how long? It's not going anywhere."

Little did Em know how wrong she would be.

Chapter Thirteen

*S*tefan considered his options. He had not lost his temper and hit anyone in fifteen years, and it was the last time he would be in trouble. He had learned his lesson and joined the military. A few years of regimented life was all it took, he learned what he needed to, got out, and went to work for a small investigation agency that conned the cons. He was the planner when they needed a logistical plan, a wild idea, or just a different perspective.

And since then he learned that the best way to beat anyone was without fists. The physical didn't get results, and he completely agreed with that philosophy. However, when Tommy told him about this guy Derek and what he was trying to pull with Em, he lost his cool, his perspective and his temper all in one shot. So back to his options, threaten or cajole, browbeat or persuade. Persuade sounded good. Stefan rarely used his stature to intimidate. At six foot three inches and one hundred ninety five pounds, he was fit. He worked out regularly and enjoyed lifting weights more than running.

He could easily lift Em, she couldn't be more than a size six. He loved her from the moment she walked into his life and his flat the day shortly after she moved in. Completely organised in her design and ideas for the remodel of the flat and brooking no change to the design, it had taken a few months of very long days of work to get it to the point where she was living comfortably in it. All the while this mess was going on she came over to his flat for coffee every morning until her kitchen was finished. Funny thing, she would cross the hall between her flat and his, but he never saw her go down the stairs after that first day. He had wanted to ask her about it, but it never seemed the right time and she never said why deftly avoiding the subject when he seemed close to asking about it. He knew that her husband had died, but she never told him how. So being the thorough and investigative kind of guy he was, he had done some research online and made a few calls to a few friends. That is how he found out that Peter was killed in an explosion at the University of California. The investigation seemed to come to a dead-end, no leads and no one claiming that they had done it for any particular reason. Stefan knew that Em was intelligent, funny, quick-witted, yet emotionally fragile when it had anything to do with Peter, and as her protector, he had every right to punch the guy who was going to cause her heartache on the nose. *Alright, he admitted to himself, a punch on the nose wasn't the smartest thing to do — but it had sure felt good.*

His musings came to an end as he noticed Derek strolling up the pavement towards the intersection that Em so loved to watch, she said it reflected the intersections of people's lives, and how many times circumstances would intersect life and change it completely.

Stefan caught him glancing up at Em's window, and he wondered how many times had Derek done that? He balled his hands then relaxed them, a habit he had when he wanted to lose unwanted energy.

Derek did not smile, he just nodded. "I know this is hard, but I don't mean Em any harm."

"Listen to me Derek, whatever you have to say to Em had better be something she will want to hear."

"It's not what you think."

"Well considering you don't have a clue what I think, that is a pretty stupid thing to say. Now get going, Em is by the window watching and I don't want her thinking I'm getting a preview."

Both men glanced up and waved.

Em waved back but the smile she so often wore did not appear.

"I'm not Peter. I'm his brother Derek."

"That's not what you told Tommy," Stefan contradicted.

"Something must have happened that he misheard - I know what I told him."

"So why did you ask him to keep it a secret?"

Em looked pointedly at Stefan. "Stefan, you're here for moral support but I'm the one with the questions. Please?"

His expression softened and he was quiet.

Sarah and Em sat on one sofa and Stefan and Derek sat on the other, untouched coffee and cakes sat on the table between.

"Derek, you have to admit this is quite strange," Em said and looked him full in the face, hoping that no one could hear her heartbeat. He was the very image of Peter, and to have Peter sitting in front of her was disconcerting, to say the least. "Peter never spoke of you," she continued.

"He wouldn't have. He didn't know about me until California — just before the accident."

Sarah was silent, unbelieving that the man in front of her might be a cousin, she laced her fingers to prevent them from tapping.

"Tell us," urged Em.

"Well, our ancestry is Italian and Scottish," Derek began.

Em raised an eyebrow. That she already knew, she knew all about Peter and nothing of this man.

"Our grandparents escaped Italy and came to stay with family in Glasgow at the start of the war. Although it wasn't easy, they had other family here, so they made it their life and our father was born here. During a visit to family in Italy, he met our mother."

"Will you quit saying our," Stefan interrupted.

Em shot him a quick look and he went quiet again.

"He met our mother," Derek repeated then continued. "They married in Italy and she became pregnant, father wanted to return to Scotland and raise the family there. He left to make arrangements when suddenly our mother went into early labour. She gave birth to twins, Peter and me, now, this is where it gets tricky. Father came back knowing our mother had given birth but not knowing that it was a set of twins, and they gave Peter to him telling him that was his son." Derek sipped the cold coffee then added, "and my grandparents kept me."

Em looked at Derek. "Because they didn't want to lose you both."

Derek returned her gaze. "Exactly. They knew that father would take us both back to Scotland and they may or may not see us both, but if they kept one son then they would have a part of their daughter to raise as their own."

"Surely the birth certificate stated that it was twins?"

"No, the birth was at home and the registration was done as one child."

"And how was your birth registered?" asked Stefan.

"My birth was registered as a…"

The house phone rang, Sarah answered it, and with a puzzled expression said, "It's for you Derek."

Surprised he took the phone. "Yes?"

Less than a minute elapsed and he hung up the phone without having said another word.

"I'm sorry, I have to leave, but we can continue this conversation another time?" He asked gazing sadly at Em.

She nodded and saw him to the door, closing it quickly to prevent any extended goodbyes. She returned to the room stating, "I am going to have a glass of white wine and do not wish to discuss any of this."

Chapter Fourteen

*E*m knocked on the door and it opened immediately.

She looked up and was about to speak when he suddenly, gently, drew her into his arms, bent his head and touch her lips with his, gentle with a passion held in check. Soon, he started to draw back but her arms went around his neck so naturally.

He whispered her name and once again his lips touched hers and she heard herself say, "kiss me as if there was no tomorrow," and he did.

Tommy knocked on Em's door and finally rang the bell. *What was going on? Was Em okay?* He never had to ring the bell. He stood there undecided with the morning rolls, coffee, bananas, doughnuts and milk.

He would ask Stefan, he always knew what to do. He knocked on the door and then pressed the bell. A very sleepy Stefan answered the door.

"Stefan, there's no answer at Em's and she's always there, and I don't know what to do. What should we do? Maybe she's hurt? Maybe we should call someone?" His words poured out in the usual rush when he was nervous or upset. Then just behind the blockade of Stefan Em peered out.

"Sorry, Tommy. I had a, um, sleepover at Stefan's," stammered Em, unsure what else to say to a shy boy of twelve.

Stefan looked at Tommy and smiled. "Tommy in a few years you'll understand, and in the meantime, you can drop everything here."

Tommy looked up at the blond giant and handed him the bag.

"Will Em be able to play chess this afternoon?"

"Yes!" came the voice from the background, strong, determined, and happy.

Em giggled; giggled like she hadn't in a long time. She felt free and twirled around in Stefan's shirt which fit her like a huge dress. It was lovely to feel warm and protected and…well, that was enough for now.

She looked at the first man she had been with in three years in a new light. She had always thought of him as a friend, and now she looked at him as a man and realised for the first time how attractive he was. Tall and blond with light blue eyes, he was large but not fat, well-built but not too hard. In fact, he was just right, because when he held her in his arms she fit just perfectly into his embrace.

Stefan caught Em's look and felt like he was sixteen again. She was beautiful like an orchid, rare and elusive, yet so loving and gentle.

"Time for a coffee dear one?"

"Yes, please."

"In a minute," he dictated and she happily agreed.

A few hours later they sat in Em's lounge with a breakfast picnic spread before them, morning rolls, scones, bacon, eggs, mushrooms, sausage, coffee and doughnuts. Soft smooth jazz played in the background and they ate their way through the feast with the winter sun shining through the front window.

Stefan sighed, he never thought that he could feel real happiness and contentment like this again. It had been so long ago.

His father had been a drinker and his mother worked, though she was not the long-suffering sort. She didn't cower, she went out into the world and made a living, but she paid a heavy price as his father's jealousies manifested into violence when he was drunk. Stefan was very young when it came to an end. He came home from school one day and she was lying on the sofa with one eye that was bruised and swollen. She had spoken to him in a gentle soft voice. "Stefan, I want you to go see Aunt Sofie and stay there for a bit." And kissed him on the forehead as she always did adding, "I love you very much." And that was the last time he saw her lovely wide-open golden smile that everyone in the neighbourhood knew so well and loved.

Obeying her he had left. He found out later that she was hurt so badly that she died moments after he left. For years he couldn't understand why. He had seen them together smiling and happy, laughing and teasing, and Stefan saw that she looked at him in a way when she thought he wasn't looking, it was a look he didn't understand. Now he understood. Whatever happened, he knew that they loved each other.

She died because he had killed her. He had hit her in the head and he had killed her. Stefan knew that he didn't mean to, that he had loved her in his own possessive way, but Stefan hated him anyway because he had taken away the beautiful mother who had loved him, and that he could never forgive, and he never did.

Stefan looked at Em. She was animated and telling him a silly story, which he wasn't following. Usually, he paid attention, but at that moment all he could think was that he had finally shared a moment with the woman he loved and that he wanted to savour it and make it last, and yes, he was going to pick up what she was saying because it was important.

Chapter Fifteen

" What?" Sarah was trying to keep herself composed and not sound too happy or shocked.

"Okay, I slept with Stefan. I don't know if you're shocked or surprised, or what?"

Sarah looked at Em over the coffee she had almost spilt.

Ummm

Ummmm what? Em asked

Sarah smiled. She couldn't help herself. She smiled so wide she thought her mouth might stretch so much it would never return to its normal shape.

She carefully put the coffee on the table and then jumped up and hugged Em.

"I am so, so happy! I mean, I thought and… I hoped and… then you were so silly, remember a few years ago you tried to… anyway, I knew that he and I wouldn't… that you would… I mean, I was just waiting and it was taking so long and then.

"Wait, hold on Sarah, you're starting to run on like Tommy."

"I am *so not* like that, he talks fast, I'm just rambling. Oh Em, you so deserve this, he loves you so much!"

"Okay, just wait a minute. I'm just totally and completely confused now because I don't know what I've just done to our relationship."

"Excuse me, whatever you have done you haven't done it by yourself, you've both done it," Sarah laughed and gave Em a sly wink.

"Yes, yes, we've both done it," Em smiled in memory.

Sarah sighed. "I am about to be very jealous."

"Why would you be jealous? You have men at least three or four deep hanging around you."

"Yes, maybe I do, but you well know it's about quality, not quantity. Anyway, this moment is not about me it is about you and, I have news!"

Once again life interrupted their conversation as the doorbell rang.

"Yes?" answered Em.

"Hello Ma'am, we are looking for a Mrs. Emily Lawson."

"You've found her."

"This is Detective Sergeant Ian Roberts. Mrs. Lawson, may we have a minute?"

She buzzed them in.

A few minutes later, with coffee and the usual biscuits on the table, Em looked at the couple in front of her, a man and woman in street clothes.

"What is this about?" Em asked.

"Mrs. Lawson, have you met a Derek Romano?" asked DS Roberts.

"Yes, I have. Why?"

"Mrs. Lawson, you were about to say?"

"Well, I just met him for the first time the other day. He was claiming to be my husband's long-lost brother. We had a brief conversation, he left early in the afternoon and I haven't seen him since. Is there a problem?"

"Yes, ma'am. I'm afraid he's been killed in a car accident, a hit and run."

Em's face lost colour. "When did this happen?"

"Just last night," the DS answered.

"And how did you find out about me?" Em caught the glance between the two visitors. "Yes?" she prompted.

"Well, Mrs. Lawson, he has quite a few photos of you in his flat and your contact details were found on his phone. We thought you may be able to shed some light on his recent movements."

"Well, I don't know much. I know he had been around for a few weeks, he mentioned it when we met."

"Would you please tell us the circumstances of this meeting?"

"As I said, he found me while trying to locate Peter, saying that he was his brother. My husband died several years ago in California and I returned to Scotland to live here, in my husband's flat. I had never met him before."

"Has anyone else met him?"

"Well I was here too, and so was Stefan, Em's neighbour," offered Sarah.

"And you live where Miss Livingstone?"

"I have a place in London and sometimes stay just around the corner."

"And Stefan, what is his last name? And where does he live?"

"His surname is Lundgren, and just across the landing," answered Em.

The detective noted this in his book and Em knew that Stefan would be getting a visit soon. She wondered how she could give him a warning.

"Is there anything else?" Em asked.

"What kind of car do you drive Mrs.Lawson?"

"I don't."

DS Roberts raised an eyebrow

Em stood. "Look, I'm very sorry to hear about Derek's death, but I only met him once and although it was recent, I really don't think that I can provide any further details."

DS Roberts and his silent partner stood. Detective Constable Miller gave Em her card. "If you should think of anything else Mrs. Lawson, please give us a call. And you said Mr Lundgren lives?"

"Just across the landing, although I don't think he's home at the moment." Em sincerely hoping that he wasn't home, she was not sure why she felt so strongly that she should speak to him first, she just did.

Sarah opened the door to show them out and pre-empted them by knocking on Stefan's door. No answer.

"If you like I can let him know to call you?" Em offered from the doorway.

"Thank you, ma'am. Goodbye."

Sarah went straight for a whiskey, and Em headed for the fridge for a glass of white wine. She was detoured from heading to the lounge with her wine by a knock on the door.

There stood Tommy holding a bag of doughnuts in his hand which he promptly offered.

"Hi Em," he said. "Is it okay to continue with our game today?"

"I'm sorry Tommy, but it's not a good day today. Sarah is here for a visit."

Tommy's young face fell and he scratched his ear.

"Okay, I'll see you tomorrow then," turning away to head down the stairs.

Em stopped him in his tracks. "I'll tell you what, since tomorrow is Saturday why don't we have a bit of play when you bring the messages in the morning, and we'll have a treat while we play?"

His face brightened. "You bet," he said and skipped down the stairs whistling as he left.

"Was that your young admirer?"

"Sarah, where do you get these ideas?"

Sarah smiled, sipped her whiskey then frowned. "Well, that wasn't what I expected."

"What did you expect? And what were you so excited about before they arrived?"

"I had a call from Alisa. She said that she got a call from Moira, remember Moira? Simon's secretary?"

"And?"

"And it turns out that Moira knows more than she let on during the visit."

Em plopped onto one sofa while Sarah settled onto the other.

Tucking her feet under her, Em sipped her wine and frowned. "Before we start trying to straighten out this mess let me call Stefan before the police talk to him."

The phone rang until it reached Stefan's voicemail. "Bother!" Em left a message requesting an immediate callback.

"Now what is it that Moira knows?"

Sarah sipped the amber liquid reflectively and continued. "Well, she called Alisa to follow up about this charity thing that she volunteered to do for Simon, and it turns out that…"

Em's phone vibrated and Sarah was interrupted once again. She rolled her eyes, decided that life would be better with more alcohol and so went for another whiskey.

Em filled in Stefan on the police visit.

"Thank's for the head's up, I'll keep it in mind. Sorry Em, I've got to head back into my meeting. I'll stop by when I get home and you can give me all the details, over dinner? My place?"

Em smiled into the phone as she agreed. Sarah returned and tried not to look smug.

"Sarah, don't start about Stefan. Now please, tell me about Moira before I explode!"

Chapter Sixteen

*E*m cut into the last portion of steak and put it into her mouth where it melted as all the others had.

"Okay Stefan, you're hired. You are the most wonderful chef."

Stefan beamed and bowed, "We live to serve. No, no, you sit," he insisted as Em started to clear away the dishes. "Dessert will be served in the lounge, and I'm sorry to say that it doesn't have the same lovely view of your own intersection that yours does."

"But it does have a lovely fire, and candles, and lovely company."

As she stood, Stefan gathered her into his arms and tilted her head back with his finger tucked under her chin. She returned his gaze and felt the warmth of his arms relax her, and even with all the upheaval that life had presented her with lately, she felt contentment.

As she lay in his arms stretched out on the sofa with a glass of port in hand, the questions returned to her.

"Stefan, what am I to do? I can't let all this go. I have to find out exactly how Peter died. Was it an accidental explosion or did someone kill him? And did Derek have anything to do with it? And did someone murder Derek, or was it really a hit-and-run accident?" She continued with the questions that overwhelmed her. "And why did Derek arrive now? I mean if he had met with Peter in San Diego why did he wait three years to find me and show up now? And —" She stopped as Stefan's arms lightly tightened around her.

"Don't worry love," he reassured her. "We'll figure it out."

Em fell silent, noting the endearment yet not knowing how to respond.

As if reading her mind, Stefan said, "I know that this is early and you don't know exactly how you feel. But I want you to know that it's okay, we are just starting this journey and I never want to do anything to spoil our friendship. Just know that I am here for you. Okay, little one?"

Em snuggled more closely into his embrace and nodded. That was enough for now.

Tommy said "check," and with a flourish moved his bishop so the king was caught no matter which way he moved.

Em raised both eyebrows, impressed. In just a few months Tommy had taken to chess like a duck to water, as the old adage went.

"I can see this is going to take a little time," she said.

Tommy wrinkled his nose. "Every time you say that it takes forever for you to move," he moaned.

"I know Tommy, but if you keep this up, you'll be too good to play with me."

"Oh no Em, that won't ever happen."

She smiled and ruffled his curly red hair and he blushed.

"Em, I've been wondering…" Tommy began.

"Yes, Tommy?"

"Maybe that lady knows something about that man Derek who was hit by the car?"

"What lady?"

"Oh, I saw him in town a couple of times and he had a lady with him." Tommy was quick to add, "Oh he wasn't holding her hand or anything, they were just usually at The Coffee Bar." Naming a popular cafe that specialised in international coffees, owned by an Italian family as Em remembered.

"Do you remember what she looked like?"

Tommy reflected. "She was short, like Sarah, and had dark hair, and she had dark eyes."

"You noticed her eyes?"

"Yes, they were dark, almost as if there was no… pupils?" he said unsure, searching for the right word. "Yeah, that's it, they were spooky. I've never seen anyone with eyes that dark. Anyway, she was little and skinny," he continued, warming to the description, "and she had a funny way of looking."

"Funny how?" prompted Em.

"She was always looking around at other people. I noticed because Ma is always telling me to pay attention when someone talks to me and not look around like I'm not paying attention, not that I don't pay attention, it's just that she thinks I don't, but I do." Tommy stopped and smiled sheepishly.

"You're doing fine," Em said, patting his hand. She thought for a moment. "Have you seen her around since that man Derek died? Has she been in the cafe again?"

Once again Tommy considered before answering. "No, I don't think so." His forehead furrowed as he thought further. "Wait a minute! Yes, I did see her just one other time. I went into the shop to buy some of the coffee Mrs. MacLean across the street likes, it's that special Greek coffee that is so strong. Yuck, she let me have a taste once and I got a whole lot of stuff in my mouth." Tommy wrinkled his nose at the memory.

At Em's prompting, Tommy continued with the story.

"She was behind the counter talking to a lady there. I remember I thought it was weird because they don't let anyone behind the counter, they have one of those counter things that swing up and down to let them in and out. Anyway, she was talking to the older lady, the one with the accent."

Em leaned forward. "Do you remember anything else about the lady she was talking to? Did either seem upset or…?"

"Oh yes, the younger one was crying and saying it wasn't her fault, and then the older lady saw me looking and took her into the back part where I couldn't see anything else."

"When was this?"

"Just a couple of days ago."

A week after the accident, Em mused. "Well let me have a little think about my next move and I'll see you tomorrow," Em said.

My next move she thought, is to go to the shop, then dammit.

As soon as she considered going out she immediately felt nauseous and her skin started to become clammy, always her physical reaction.

"Sarah, can you do me a favour? How about stopping at the Coffee Bar this afternoon on your way over?" She went on to explain the conversation with Tommy and her idea. "Would you mind?"

"Of course not, and I'll fill you in on my conversation with Alisa tonight. What's on the menu for dinner?"

"You'll have to put up with my cooking I'm afraid. Stefan said an assignment has come up and he'll be down in London for a few days."

"Maybe we could order in?"

"Sarah you're welcome to the kitchen, create one of your fabulous meals and I'll clean up."

"Deal."

Stefan felt guilty about lying to Em, but he couldn't tell her everything, yet. Soon, but not yet.

"James, what have you found out?"

"This Derek guy has only been in the country for a few months. He has two passports, one American and one EU, issued in Italy. The Italian is in the name of Derek Romano, and the American..."

"Yes, the American?"

"Is in the name of Peter Lawson."

"What?"

"We did a thorough search in the flat he was renting, we weren't the first, but we were definitely tidier. Someone else was searching for something, and I don't know if they found it or not, but they did leave it in a bit of a mess."

"Wonder what they were looking for?"

They sat in silence for a minute

"Have you found out anything about the car that hit him?" Stefan asked.

"Yes, it was reported stolen the day before the hit-and-run, around the corner from where you live. As a matter of fact, the police are working on their suspect list, I don't know how to break it to you, but you're on it," James smiled, tented his fingers and tutted.

"You would like that," Stefan commented. "What exactly are they basing it on, strictly proximity? Oh right, and the fact that I punched him. They called again the other day and I left a message that I was conveniently out of town on business, but I can't avoid them forever."

Stefan rubbed his forehead. *What would he tell them? He'd think about it soon.*

"Let me know when the car turns up."

"It has," James said. "Just this morning. It's burned up and they're working on it now, but I'd say it's the same car, they'll just be confirming." James made a pyramid of his fingers and tutted again.

No wonder his men call him King Tut, Stefan thought.

Stefan settled himself in the chair across the desk from Detective Sergeant Ian Roberts and his assistant, Detective Constable Miller.

"Thank you for coming Mr. Lundgren," began Detective Roberts.

"Anything I can do to help."

"Well, you know that we are looking into the death of Derek Romano?"

"Yes."

"What can you tell me about him?"

"What would you like to know?"

"How well did you know him?"

"Not well, only met him a couple of times."

"And?"

"I know that you know the first time I met him there was a slight…altercation," Stefan stated. "It was a misunderstanding really. Anyway, we got it sorted out and then I met him once after that."

"Yes, we understand that he visited your neighbour Emily Lawson?"

"True."

"What can you tell us about the meeting?"

"He said he knew her husband and wanted to express condolences about his death," Stefan answered.

"Three years later?"

Stefan just returned his gaze.

"Let's stop messing about. Exactly what was said during the visit?"

"Didn't Em— Emily, tell you?"

"Yes, but we'd like to hear it from you."

"He said he was her dead husband's brother."

"And she had never met him before?"

"Not that I am aware of. He was a long-lost brother and had just tracked her down when looking for Peter, the flat originally belonged to him when Em moved in. We had coffee and biscuits and that was it."

"And he left on good terms?"

"Yes."

"So why had you attacked him several days earlier?"

"As I said, it was an altercation due to a misunderstanding on my part about him. Unfortunately, I lost my temper, something I am not prone to doing."

Stefan rubbed his chin

"I am sorry Detective Roberts, it was a short simple meeting. Does it have to do with his death?"

"Well, of course, we're looking into it. The car that hit him was stolen, but then you already know that don't you."

Stefan looked surprised. "Why would I know that?"

Detective Roberts smiled thinly.

"Thank you for your time today Mr Lundgren. We'll be in touch when we have more questions."

"Anytime," said Stefan, standing and towering above the other two. He extended his hand, which they took.

After the door closed Ian turned to his colleague. "What do you think Marie?"

"He knows more than he's saying, I think they all do. Which makes me wonder what is going on?"

"I know. I have a feeling it's got something to do with the husband's death."

"What makes you think so?" Marie asked.

"Just a feeling. It was an explosion under suspicious circumstances that killed him and left the widow with a small fortune. She moved back to his flat and from several interviews has never left."

"How strange. She doesn't look like a hermit."

Ian steepled his hands and looked through them, he liked to say that it gave him a different perspective, looking closely at a detail and then back to the bigger picture.

"I wonder why she never leaves the flat?" he asked.

"I have a friend who is a psychologist," Marie offered. "One time we were talking about the different problems people have, one of them is called agoraphobia. It's where people don't leave the place they live."

"Why are they afraid of going out into the world?"

"Well, contrary to popular belief it's more defined than that. It's more a fear of not being able to handle a particular situation, or handle whatever it is they are afraid of and they don't want to be out in the world, so they go out less and less, avoiding the fear until they finally just stop going out. For example, if you were really afraid of dogs and feel faint when you have seen one, then if you stay home you avoid the fear."

"Dogs?"

"Just an example sir. It could be anything, but it's more about the reaction to the phobia than the phobia itself."

"Interesting. I wonder what it is that our Mrs. Lawson is afraid of?"

"What shall I cook for you, Stefan?"

"Seriously Em, come over and I'll cook."

"Oh yes Stefan, I am coming over and providing the dinner. You've been so good."

Stefan smiled into the phone. He knew Em didn't like to cook and somehow that was part of her charm.

"Duck," he said.

"Duck?"

"Yes"

"Alright, we're set then. Okay just leave the flat open and I'll take care of the rest?"

"Absolutely," said Stefan, then added, "Should I notify the fire department?"

"Oh funny!"

"Em, I'll be back at seven and be ready for eight."

"Perfect." Em pressed end on the mobile and smiled to herself. Sarah looked up from the magazine she was pretending to read, working hard not to smile.

"You are incorrigible," commented Em, heading to put the kettle on for tea.

"Me?" Sarah asked with an innocent wide-eyed expression on her face.

Em pulled out the teapot and put three bags in it. As she waited for the kettle to boil, she wondered. "What do we need to know and how do we find out about it?"

"You know Peter was my cousin and I adored him as long as I knew him, but it wasn't long, remember, we met as teenagers and he didn't like to talk about his childhood. He was focused on school, his dad had died and he came to live with us for a couple of years. He was sixteen or seventeen."

"Did you ever meet his dad?"

Sarah scrunched her eyes as she thought. "Once I think when I was very small. Our dads were brothers, Peter's father was older and they hadn't been very close growing up. Uncle Robert was a bit controlling and Dad just didn't seem to want to talk about it either. Seems the men in my family don't talk very much, but it seems to work out okay because the women make up for it."

Em poured the tea and blew on it before sipping. "You're right, your mom definitely likes to talk. Now I know where you get it from!"

Sarah tugged at Em's hair. "Back to family discussion."

"Okay. Well, when Peter and I met he was on a research trip and was giving some guest lectures."

"You are not going to tell me the story again," Sarah said, trying to sound bored.

"No! Now, they thought that the explosion might have had something to do with his nuclear research, but couldn't prove it or figure it out because he was working on getting rid of the waste and the environmentalists were supporting him, and —" She stopped.

"You okay?" asked Sarah.

"Yeah, I'm fine. I just can't believe that I can talk about this now. God, it used to hurt so much to even think about losing him."

"It has been three years."

"I know, but I loved him so intensely for so long."

Sarah sipped and nodded. "Where's the cookies?"

"Never mind," Em said changing the subject, "and they're in the cookie jar of course. Anyway, what do we know about that day?"

Sarah returned from the kitchen chewing on her cookie. "Moira said that Derek was seen in the vicinity about half an hour before the explosion. What time did Peter arrive?"

"About two p.m., and he was due back about three or four. Sarah, do you think it was an accident?"

Sarah hesitated before answering. "No, I don't think so. But the investigation ended, I came over here with you and just kind of let it go."

"Do you think we should look into it?"

Another hesitation, then, "Yes, I do, and for a couple of reasons. It will give closure, to both of us, and then maybe you can get on with your life ... a bit more. Maybe it will even help you to get out more."

"How so?"

"Well, I've done a little research into this —"

"So have I," said Em.

"—and I think that once you find out what it is you're afraid of out there, then you'll be able to address it and then go out into the world."

"Don't you think I've not thought of that? I mean, I would love to go out for walks and parties and travel again and see people, but it's just always been so comfortable here."

"And now? "

"Well, it's as if this flat is my comfort blanket and that as long as I'm here I'll be safe, and I won't lose anything."

"You mean like Peter and the baby?" Sarah asked.

"Yes. If I don't put myself out there then I can't be hurt here," Em said, placing her hand on her heart.

Em was ready for dinner early and stood at the window just in time to see Mrs. McLean taking her cat out for a walk with the garish pink collar and leash.

She sipped the dry martini, eyeing the last olive in the bottom of the glass. Three olives made the perfect martini.

As she viewed the intersection she realised that she had missed a few days of her regular routine of watching the passersby over the last few weeks. It had been such a ritual, every morning and afternoon.

Partly, she realised that they were no longer remote and could not be controlled by her imagination. Derek had been down in the intersection and now he was gone too, killed by a hit and run driver.

She had thought she could be safe in here but was slowly coming to the realisation that one cannot be safe from life itself. Over the last three years, there had been a gradual change. At first, she was committed to making the flat everything that Peter wanted it to be, then she was content to just spend time in it, watching people pass through the intersection, which as such was a reflection on life. Then writing the stories of their lives as she imagined them. Once again though, real life had touched her.

Derek looked so much like Peter it was eerie, in fact, it went further than that. She remembered that at the time there was something that shook her, it was the way he reached up and tugged on his earlobe when he was thinking about something. Peter had done this, and she had surprised him once when he was thinking, just when she thought he would, she had reached over and gently tugged on his lobe. Surprised but pleased he reached over and gently tugged her earlobe and that had become their silent gesture when they were just content and didn't have to speak.

Thinking about it more thoroughly, there was one point in the conversation with Derek when she could have sworn he was looking at her and then her earlobe, and it had given her a shiver. But he had not reached out to touch her, and yet she had a feeling that he was thinking about it.

Em sighed. With all of the recent emotional roller coaster she realised that now she could think about Peter without her heart beating a new rhythm in her chest, and the memories were all sweet.

"You do make the perfect martini," Stefan said sipping the ice-cold drink.

"Thank you, kind sir," Em nodded and sipped her own.

"Dinner will be ready in about half an hour Emily," said Douglas of *Dinner at Eight*, the company who provided all the catering for Em's dinner parties.

He wore a crisp white chef uniform and was formal in his address. It had taken a full year for Em to get him to call her Emily instead of Mrs. Lawson, and it was only because of the hollow threat that she would stop using him for catering.

"Thank you, Douglas. I believe the table is set?"

"I have already done that for you, Emily, there is a complete set of dishes here. May I compliment you Mr Lundgren?"

"Thank you, Douglas, and please, call me Stefan so I don't feel left out."

"Certainly sir."

"It took me a year Stefan, and you expect Douglas to call you by your first name after just one meeting? Such sacrilege!"

Stefan smiled and dropped his arm around Em's shoulders. "I am very persuasive."

Em smiled contentedly as she rested in the curve of his arm. "You certainly are."

"Now tell me, what have you and Sarah been up to?"

"Not sure how to begin." Em took another sip of the drink, savouring the flavour and taking another moment to dig out one of the olives.

"Well, we've decided to do a little investigation."

"Of?"

"Peter's death. I know it seems strange after all this time, but it's partly because of Derek and his visit and then his death. And Sarah feels it will give me some kind of closure and may help me to…"

"Go out into the world?" Stefan finished.

"Yes."

"Whatever will help you. Now, what can I do to help?"

"I don't suppose you have any contacts in the photography world who know about investigating?" Em asked jokingly.

"I do happen to have a few friends who look into situations."

Em turned her head to look at him and almost spilled her drink. "What?"

"Well I do have a wide range of friends and they are happy to help, most of the time. I just need to consider who is best suited to this."

"How can they look into something a world away?"

"One never knows," Stefan said, trying to sound mysterious.

Douglas came out of the kitchen. "Dinner is now served in the dining room, Emily."

Her mouth began to water as she thought of the lovely duck dinner they were about to enjoy.

"We will continue this conversation after dinner," she said.

🐝

She looked at her hands, difficult to see in the dark, but not impossible. She had always been good at that, they had always said she had cat's eyes.

The key slipped into the lock and she went through the door, careful to close it silently.

In her bare feet, she made no noise.

Remembering the layout of the flat, she cut to the right and headed into the bedroom, surprised to see no one there.

She never went out. Where could she be?

Then, remembering the lights in the flat across the hall she considered the options. It was better this way. She just needed to start the fire and let it do the work, better that the flat was empty, better because there would be more suffering than if it was quick, and oh how she wanted her to suffer.

Silently she pulled the materials from the bag and set them out. Wouldn't take much for a big bang and a lot of fire. Who said education was a bad thing? It just depended upon the topic of education.

The thin lips tilted up in the corner. Most satisfactory.

She closed and locked the door behind her and thought that fifteen minutes was just enough time. Just enough.

೮ঙ৮ূ

Chapter Seventeen

*E*m stood in the middle of the wreckage that had once been her comfortable, cosy home and let the tears run down her face. It felt like losing Peter all over again. Everything that she had built and decorated, everything she had done just the way he'd wanted it to be. And here it was, burned and destroyed.

In the watery light of the morning sun, the jagged edges of broken furniture cut silhouettes in the ashes of the floor. The master bedroom was a pile of rubble and the small room that had held the trunk of photos was destroyed.

Crossing her arms, she was thankful that she'd decided to show the photos to Stefan last night after dinner and that he'd lugged the entire trunk and the smaller case next to it into his flat, otherwise, those would have been destroyed too.

The firemen had left about an hour before daylight and declared the bedroom and entire front side off limits and had said that the entire flat would have to be checked and she was allowed only into the hall.

The smoke permeated the entire flat, and Em felt her shoulders sag.

"What you won't do to move in with me," Stefan said lightly behind Em. She turned and looked up at him. He had been so strong and was trying to make her feel better. She shook her head and said nothing, but did not resist when he pulled her into an embrace.

A moment later they heard, "What the hell?" as Sarah arrived at the top of the stairs.

Stefan caught her as she tried to fly into the room to see.

Em turned and hugged Sarah. "I'm okay," then repeated. "I'm okay."

"You had better be! I'm not ready to lose my best friend!"

"Come on you two," Stefan commanded as he led both Em and Sarah to his flat.

Ensconced on the sofa, Sarah demanded to know what happened.

"We had dinner last night and were looking over the photos in the trunk and we heard the explosion, and then the fire just seemed to engulf the front of the flat and we couldn't get anywhere near it. Thank heavens the firemen arrived as quickly as they did, I don't know how far it would've gone."

"Thank God you weren't in the house."

"I know Sarah, I would've been toast."

"As it is, you're merely smudged," Sarah said pointing at a spot on Em's face. Em wiped her cheek and felt some ashes that she must have picked up from something in the front hall.

"You'll just have to stay with me."

Em blanched. "Oh, Sarah I want to, I really, really do. I just can't."

At that moment Stefan's mobile rang. Before answering he said, "You're not going anywhere Em, you're staying right here, and don't even think of arguing. Either of you." And with that he left the room, slamming the door to his bedroom shut.

Sarah raised an eyebrow. "He is bigger than you," she observed.

"Yes, and stronger — and in this particular case right."

Stefan worked to keep his voice lowered. "I don't care who is working on what, I want Will and John over here in the next hour. I want samples of everything from that explosion and then I want them analysed in comparison with that explosion that killed Peter. And I want a man over here to keep an eye on Em when I'm not here."

"What if she tries to leave?" James asked over the phone.

"Don't worry about that. Also, I want a check on everyone in the building."

"Oh, let's not stop there, why not everyone within a mile?"

"Don't get smart with me James."

James tutted into the phone.

"I know when Franco is coming in to visit across the street," Stefan said.

Silence reigned for about a minute.

"Alright," James sighed into the phone. "I'll have to make a few calls to find out about the contents of the explosion in California, that's a bit tricky."

"I know you can do it."

"Will and John will be there shortly. When is Franco coming?"

"Sooner than you think," Stefan said and ended the call.

When he returned to the lounge Em was sat curled up in the corner near the window that had a street view.

Her gaze shifted to Stefan. "Sarah went out to get some clothes and a few sundries for my new place." Attempting a smile she asked, "Do you mind if I borrow the guest room?"

"Whatever will make you comfortable," Stefan said disappointed.

"It's just, I feel like I'm invading and I'm not ready to do that. I want — I need — to have my own corner to curl into. Do you understand?" She looked directly into his light blue eyes, so tenderly that he just pulled her into his arms and enfolded her into his embrace.

"I do understand, that it's part of you and what you need, and that's all I really need to know."

She snuggled in and felt the steady beat of his heart.

"Are you going to tell me what you're up to?" she asked, slightly muffled against his chest.

"What makes you think I'm up to something?"

She leaned her head back and looked up at him. "I've lived across from you for three years and been your friend almost all that time, yet I'm only starting to get to know you, but I am now. So, are you going to tell me what you're up to?"

He shook his head. "No, not yet. Let me see what I can find out first, then I'll share it with you. Okay?"

"I find those to be acceptable terms —for now."

A short time later Sarah returned with a few sundry items stating the rest would arrive later."

"Sarah, did you talk to Alisa yet?"

"Yes, and she's sending the box to us overnight. To be honest I'll be surprised if she doesn't hand-deliver it herself, I mean you should have heard her on the phone, she was in full nosiness Alisa on-an-adventure-mode."

Answering the knock at the door, she heard Em ask over her shoulder, "And how would Alisa visit us? I'm four flights up."

"It's called a fireman's lift Em," answered the beautiful woman at the door.

Em turned and ran to the entrance to hug her unexpected visitor. "What are you doing here Alisa!?"

"That's a nice greeting! And what are you doing getting your house blown up?"

"Sorry, I love that you're here, I just can believe it, and it's only partly blown up."

"Well, we decided to come for a couple of reasons. It's mostly you, but we have rolled a London trip into it. Gray had some meetings and I wanted to come here, so we compromised. He brought me here and he's taken the jet and headed down to London. He'll be back in a few days, so I'll check into the…"

"You will do nothing of the kind," interrupted Sarah. "You'll stay with me. It's not huge, but it's on the ground floor and filled with lovely bottles of white wine and good company."

"Are you sure?"

"I insist. Besides, I have some new sketches for you to look at."

Alisa agreed and they settled in the lounge for a catch-up.

William and John were the two best explosives experts at the agency and hated being interrupted for fieldwork as they were working on a new chemical breakdown of a seemingly undetectable explosive.

Grudgingly, they headed over to Roberts Street.

"I thought you were going to stop smoking John?" Will asked as he opened the window for fresh air.

"I was, but Nina left me over the weekend and it's been too stressful. I'll quit next week," he answered, taking a long drag.

Short and wiry with slicked-back hair and a thin tie accompanying his suit, John looked like a retro *Man from Uncle* character. Will was only slightly taller but quite round and tended to wear loose-fitting suits with his tie habitually loosened. As a bachelor, he often thought how lucky he was to have the freedom to do as he wished. His cleaning lady came twice a week and with his love of cooking, he had a good life without a wife.

"Couldn't they have sent the other team out for this? Why did they have to pull us? I really think we're close to breaking this new formula." John grumbled as he turned the car onto Roberts Street.

"I heard Stefan called in a favour, the address is a flat across from his. Maybe it was just too close to home."

They pulled up to see Stefan come around the corner of his building, looking up toward one of the top window flats. He glanced up once more and hoped that Em was busy and not paying attention to this intersection she so loved to watch, although his window was slightly further away and would have a slightly smaller perspective.

Will and John pulled their cases from the car and Stefan led them up the stairs, filling them in as they went.

"The explosion occurred last night about eleven o'clock, the owner was out of the flat, and obviously won't be back until it's been released and cleaned up."

"Why did you ask for us?" Will asked.

"Because you two are the best, also, there's a slant to this. There was an explosion in California about three years ago, at a University, and I want you to tell me if you think it might be the same person."

"Why?" they asked in unison, which they did often much to the chagrin of the person they were speaking to.

"I'm not entirely sure, it may just be a hunch but there is a relation between the two, and I just don't like coincidences. Get the details of this, I'm working on getting the information on the explosion at the University, then have the two compared."

"We'll look into it for similarities," John said. "Bombers do tend to have a signature, just not sure if two are enough for a pattern, especially since they're so far apart. Why stop for three years in the middle?"

"I'm not sure they have. They may just have done other jobs," said Stefan, "and they have been far enough apart geographically for no one to pick up a pattern. So if you find any similarities then we'll be able to do a database search."

Once reaching the top of the stairs Stefan showed them the door, removing the tape for them to enter.

Just at that moment, his door opened and Sarah stepped out.

Stefan stepped aside, quickly shutting the door.

She looked up at him. "What are you up to? What's going on?"

"Just checking to make sure everything is secure and there aren't any people here who shouldn't be."

"You know if you're going to start lying…" Sarah warned.

"Just don't ask any questions I can't answer and I won't have to lie," Stefan said coolly and changed the subject. "How's Em doing?"

"Fine, she's talking to Alisa who's come for a visit." Sarah decided not to divulge any more and asked "Are you going out or coming in? Because if you're going out could I ask for a lift?"

"Sure, no problem. Where to?"

"There are a couple of things that Em needs that I forgot to get. By the way, how are you doing with all of this? If I didn't know better I'd say that you arranged this just to get Em into your house," Sarah said.

"But you do know better," Stefan answered.

"Yes. I think so," she said, reflecting on whether she really did or not.

"When you come back, why don't I make dinner for all of us?"

"Great idea. We can get the food while we're out."

"Are you sure you're okay?" Alisa asked Em when Sarah was out the door.

"I'm doing okay considering. Thanks for coming Alisa, I didn't expect this."

"Of course I would come, you know I would do that as soon as Sarah called. I know we haven't been as close as but you must know that whenever you needed, I mean really needed, me I would be here? Seriously! How long have we been friends?"

"I know, and to answer your question I think it's going on twenty-one years. Wasn't it the second or third year of school? You were stunning even then, which is completely ridiculous at seven years old!"

"Maybe, but if it hadn't been for you I never would've passed Math."

"And if it hadn't been for you Alisa, I would probably still be…"

"Be…?"

"I was going to say I'd still be in California. I mean, if we hadn't gone to that lecture where I met Peter, I don't know where I would be."

Alisa wheeled next to the sofa and deftly moved from chair to couch. "What does a girl have to do to get a glass of wine here?"

Em's eyes refocused. "Ah, the price is high. I would love to see the contents of the box you brought with you, and I am happy to supply cheese and other munchies with the wine. Red or white?"

"Red for me, and would you please bring the box from the door and we can devour it and the goodies at the same time."

One hour later the bottle of red was dwindling, a few crumbles of cheese and biscuits remained, and papers were starting to litter the table and floor

Alisa sat back and looked at Em from over the rim of her glass. "Em, do you hate me very much?" she asked.

"What? Why ever would you think that?"

"Because of Peter. I convinced you to go to the lecture so I could see Grayson, and I didn't want to go alone."

Em regarded her lifelong friend and couldn't keep back the tears. "Oh, my dearest Alisa. I would not trade one instant of my life with Peter, even with the heartache that followed."

"But you left so quickly."

Em reached out and gently took Alisa's hand. "I did the only thing I could do at the time to handle it. The loss was so acute — and then the baby. I just had to get away to be… with Peter, or more precisely the memories of Peter, and while we had only spent a little time here during a visit we loved it so very much, And then he had carefully designed everything. I thought that if I came here and didn't leave, I could live my life through memories and …"

"..And through the people that pass through the intersection? Sarah told me how you imagine their lives."

Em smiled softly. "Yes, and their lives are all happy, at least in my imagination they are. Except of course for Mrs. McLean's cat. No cat on a leash can be a happy cat." She hesitated before continuing. "I have always been grateful to you for persuading me to go and I shall always be grateful for that. Peter and I shared so much happiness in such a short period of time, just over a year, but in that year I had a lifetime's worth of joy. Do you remember, Alisa, when I was little and Aunt Jenny would be upset about something and I would hide out in the attic, or the bedroom closet?"

"Yes?"

"Well, this is my grown-up hideout."

"But eventually you came out of the attic or the closet."

"Only because Uncle Bill would come and coax me out, or I'd still be there yet," she said and they both laughed.

"Seriously though Em, you did come out."

"And I will eventually have to leave here also. I've been driven from my home, I suppose I'll have to go further out into the world and see how far the street of my intersection goes. But not right now. Right now I'd like to know, where did you get all this?"

"The ever-efficient Moira came to the rescue. It seems that there was an old office supply storage room with some seldom-used lockers. After we visited Dean Simon, she went to investigate to see what was left and one of the lockers contained Peter's research, private notes, photos and this old box."

Alisa pulled out a box inlaid with a variety of woods. Rectangular in shape, it had no keyhole and no apparent way of opening it.

"Oh! It's a Chinese puzzle box," said Em, running her hands over the box.

"How do you get into it?" Alisa asked.

"Excellent question - I haven't a clue. One as exquisite as this must have been a unique design. I remember Peter had one that was similar. He used to joke that he kept the secrets of his life in it and if I ever figured out the combination I'd know them all."

Alisa leaned closer to get a better look. "It's so beautiful." The inlaid design was made of different coloured woods, from a dark pine to a blond beechwood. "How do they get the different woods to fit so well?"

"It all has to do with the craftsman, some are just a few pieces of wood pieced together and have a trick to opening it, while others have springs, dowels, bullets, pins and sliders. Peter loved to create them as a relaxation." Em ran her fingers lovingly over the patterned box.

"Now all we need to do is to figure out how to open this."

"Open what?" asked Sarah, who had just walked through the door, arms loaded with groceries and other miscellaneous items from one of the nearby boutique stores.

"Oh my angel!" exclaimed Em. "More clothes and food!"

Stefan followed closely behind, loaded down ever further and followed close by Tommy, who could barely be seen under his load.

Depositing his packages in the kitchen, Tommy ran back to hug Em.

Brushing away his tears he asked, "Are you sure you're okay Em? I mean it's a mess."

"How do you know?" Em started.

"From the street, you can see all the black surrounding the window and the window isn't there anymore, it's all blocked off with wood, and it's all streaky and shuttered, and you can't see anything from up here just from the street and it looks just awful," he hiccupped as he finished.

Sitting down, Em looked him squarely in the face. "I am perfectly fine," she said. "I was visiting Stefan here when it happened, so there is nothing to worry about."

"But what was it?"

Stefan walked in just at that moment and answered for her. "We don't know yet Tommy, but we'll find out, and in the meantime, Em is going to stay with me and I promise you that I will take good care of her, okay?"

Tommy looked up at the tall blond man who was so gentle and kind to Em. "It's okay with me," he nodded giving his permission.

"Good, now that's settled, I'm starving, who's for dinner?"

Tommy hugged Em once more and said "Em I have to go, but what shall I do about tomorrow's delivery? Do you still want your rolls and stuff?"

Em exchanged a glance with Stefan who nodded.

"Yes, Tommy I'd love to have you bring my rolls as you always do, and maybe even some doughnuts for a special treat."

"Sure! And chess, maybe tomorrow?"

"Well, we'll have to see, I don't have my set to play with."

Stefan broke in, "But I have one and I'll bring it out. I'll be out early tomorrow anyway, I have a couple of meetings in the centre of town."

"Cool," Tommy said, running for the door, happy that his world with Em was still okay even if it had moved location.

"That's very sweet of you Stefan."

"No problem, it should come out once in a while just to get dusted off."

"I didn't know you played."

"Not very much, I used to play with my mother when I was young. She was very good." Stefan smiled at the memory, which changed to sadness, and then his face closed. "Once again, who's for dinner?" There was a unanimous decision.

Em turned to Alisa. "Shall we pack up and start again tomorrow?"

"Perfect."

"Let's keep the box out though, it looks so pretty."

Em looked at Stefan. "Fine by me," he said. "It will actually fit well with the chess set, it's made with similar wood."

☙

"Dammit," she muttered as she sucked the blood from the cut on her finger.

She surveyed the box and decided a hammer would be the best way to go. But she hated the idea of breaking the only gift Peter had ever given her, even if she did hate him.

Her skinny fingers curled around the wooden inlaid box.

Adding insult to injury, the explosion hadn't killed that bitch Lawson.

Throwing the box on the bed she turned to sit at the kitchen table. The soiled linoleum floor curled around the edges and matched her bitter smile.

But this wasn't the end, she would find a way. It would just take a while longer, not too long though, she didn't have that much time left. But still, there was time enough.

She looked at her watch. Better leave now if she is to meet the client, she thought. She needed this job to pay for her own little enterprise.

Pulling on the heavy sweater she covered her skinny frame and felt the warmth ease her sore muscles, each day was more challenging, but she would make sure there was enough time.

ⵣ

Chapter Eighteen

*P*icking through the mess that had once been Em's comfortable bedroom, Will and John silently worked the room from opposite sides to meet in the middle. They had always done this, worked from opposite ends toward the epicentre of the explosion. They had worked as a team with the agency for five years but had been a team for ten years before that. No one ever broke them up, they worked too well together.

Nearing the centre John asked, "So what do you think?"

"I can't see any chemical residue. I've taken quite a few samples, but I don't know."

"It caused a fire, but I don't see any sign of an incendiary."

"I know, very weird."

"What are these little doughy balls?"

"Not sure, I found a few here and there. Doesn't seem to make sense, there's no pattern and they should have evaporated from the heat of the fire."

John's face beamed with delight. "Do you think we've got a new one?"

"Maybe," said Will, bending over to take one more ball as a sample.

John, delighted at the prospect of a new type of explosive, walked to what used to be a long closet.

Peering down the length of it he saw a glint in the reflection of his flashlight, gingerly stepping over the jagged edges he made his way to the end of the closet.

"Hey Will, look what I found."

Will tucked the last vial into the case and headed toward John, and at that moment the case and all its contents exploded in a mini-explosion, enough to push the rotund Will into his partner and sprawling them across the tiny entrance.

"What the hell happened over there?" Stefan asked as he dabbed disinfectant onto John's cut hand.

"Ouch, be gentle."

"A doctor's going to have to take these splinters out."

"Stefan, I know that and you're probably not helping," John said, pushing his hand away.

John and Will were in Stefan's front lounge, surrounded by Em, Sarah and Alisa, with Stefan towering over them all.

The commotion brought with it a flurry of questions.

"What happened?"

"What were you doing there?"

"Do we notify the police?"

"Are you alright?"

"I've called the doctor."

"Stop already, I can't hear when you are all talking!" John spurted out, looking to Stefan for help.

Will walked in from the kitchen with a large scotch in his right hand and sunk into the armchair.

"Stefan, didn't you have the place screened before we got there?"

"I didn't think of it, the firemen had already been through it."

"And I would say lucky not to have been blown up too. This is something new, it's got some kind of delay reaction time within it."

Sarah buzzed the doctor in and came back to fuss over John.

"Let's get you taken care of first and then we'll hear the explanations," said Em then looking at Stefan added. "And they had better be good."

The doctor bandaged John's hand and dictated that he was to go to the hospital immediately, as was Will. Stefan had made his escape by driving them both to the hospital, arriving back home after Sarah and Alisa had left and Em had gone to bed.

❤

"Look, if you want the job done it's going to cost you. I don't have time for this, so meet my price or go somewhere else."

The alley was quiet except for the rustling of a cat going through the dustbins.

The passing of a car down on the street gave a brief flash of light.

"Alright, alright, but it's got to be done tonight. Are you sure you can handle this? I mean, your father would have—"

"Don't talk to me about my father," she snapped. "You know nothing about him. It will be done tonight, and I expect the balance of the money to be in my account within one hour of notification."

A brief nod then he turned away the limp minimised with the use of the well-worn cane. He stopped and turning back said, "remember my employer..."

"I don't care," she spat out. "Just make sure I get my money, you'll be satisfied." Another nod, and he continued down the alley and disappeared into the night.

She rubbed the aching knuckle of her left hand. The job came none-to-soon. Just what she needed, a quick influx of cash.

She kicked the garbage can and the cat leapt out. Sorry for a second, she looked at the thin frame of the animal.

"Don't worry you'll find more food soon," and she too walked down the alley to disappear into the frosty night.

❤

"Stefan go to the neighbours, just for a little while, it's okay," said his mom, smiling her large hazel eyes cloudy with unshed tears. "Now you go and I'll see you later."

He bent and kissed the smooth white forehead as she lay on the couch, not noticing the blood that had gathered behind her head.

She smiled again. "And I expect you to pass all your exams next week, okay? For me?"

"Always mum, always." And as he turned to wave at her the blood came and Stefan awoke with a start.

He hadn't had that dream in a while. He wiped the sweat from his brow and got up.

Walking into the lounge he noticed the small figure curled into the corner of the sofa, of course, it was the nearest to the window with a view of the street.

Turning she asked, "Did I wake you?"

"No, just a dream."

He noticed the sweet smell of chocolate.

"I hope you don't mind, I made a hot chocolate."

"Sounds good, mind if I join you?"

"I'd love it."

A few minutes later he sat on the adjacent sofa and a moment later the moon came from behind the cloud and bathed the room in a muted light.

"I wanted to —" he started.

"Did you —" she started at the same time, and they both laughed.

"You go first," Em said.

"I wanted to tell you that I wish for you to stay here no matter how long it takes with your place."

"Thank you."

"I mean, I don't want you to feel that you have to rush anything. It's wonderful having you here and I…" his voice faded off and he took a sip of his hot chocolate before continuing. "Em, I know that a lot has happened recently, and we haven't had a chance to talk, but I want you to know…that, I…"

"Stefan, you don't have to say anything," Em said as she tucked both legs under her.

"But I want to. I've fallen in love with you, and I know that for you it might just be a complication, but know that I am here for you."

Em got up and crossed over to the couch he was on and curled up next to him. "Stefan," she began, "I am so lucky, you're a wonderful man." She felt his breathing slow. "And you are also right, I don't know how I feel, I've been tied up with Peter for such a long time and I'm just starting to deal with losing him. It's almost as if time stood still for nearly three years and that life would go on like that forever."

She turned toward him and looked up. "But you have made me see a new and fresh side to life. I'm not living so much through those who walk through that intersection outside, but I have something more, an intersection in my own life. Do you know why I enjoy watching those who pass through the street?" not waiting for an answer Em continued. "Because that intersection represents the choices and changes we all experience. If we turn this corner it leads to a different destination. When we come to an intersection we are faced with a choice, and the decision we make affects where we end up. Now I have come to an intersection and must make a choice, and all I can ask is for you to have patience with me. Please, let me discover how I feel and decide which direction I should take. Can you do that? For me?"

"Of course I can." He pulled her close and brushed her forehead with his lips, breathing a sigh of relief that she hadn't closed the door on a future.

"Now I have another favour to ask you," Em said.

"Yes? What's that?"

"Will you tell me about you?"

"What do you mean?"

"I know that you're a photographer and you go on assignments, but so much more goes on, and the fact that you know men like John and Will, explosive investigators? Is that normal in your industry?"

"Well..."

"And although we talk a lot, I still don't know very much about you. Where you grew up? Do you have brothers and sisters? Do your mom and dad live near here? Have you ever been married?"

"Wow, have you been saving up these questions?"

"Yes, as a matter of fact, I have."

"Well, I grew up in Inverness, at least until I was nine. I have a baby sister seven years younger. My mom and dad are both dead and no, I have never been married."

Hesitating, she said, "I'm sorry about your mom and dad."

"It was a long time ago," he said with a sigh and pulled her closer.

She melted into his embrace and they stayed just like that for a while.

"It's a part of who I am," he said, "and I don't ever talk about it."

Em lay still and waited for him to continue.

"My parents had known each other since they were children, they'd grown up together and had always been together. My father was gentle and loving and wanted to be a painter. My mother was smart and went to school to be a teacher. He was helping on his father's farm one day and there was an accident and he was hit on the head. He recovered, but after that, he started drinking, and he drank more and more until he was a functioning alcoholic. They loved each other so much, but when he was drunk he would just lose it and at first, he would just rant and rave and then he got worse." Stefan stopped and drew a long ragged breath before continuing. "And then he hit her. It was small at first, a slap, then another." Stefan stopped again and covered his eyes with his free hand as he remembered. Then he pulled his hand away and looked down at Em.

"You know, you kind of remind me of her. She was beautiful with large blue eyes, and long curly blonde hair, she was petite and so full of life and love. Everyone that knew her loved her sense of humour, and that is what started to make it even worse. My father withdrew into himself and he couldn't paint anymore. Mom went to work and dad became jealous of anything that took her away from him. Whenever she was home he was okay, but when she would go out to work he would start drinking, which wasn't every day but most days, and by the time she got home he would be either sleeping or just vicious."

"Why didn't she leave him?" Em asked.

"I don't know," said Stefan. "I know it sounds unbelievable, but I think that she thought that if she stayed she could change him back to the way he was, before the injury. She always remembered what he was like before and always told stories of how loving and gentle he was. Then one day I came home from school and she was on the sofa, just lying there looking so tired. She told me to go to the neighbours and play there for a while. She was so white, I should have known, I should have known but I didn't. He'd hit her so hard on the head, it caused a brain haemorrhage and killed her. I should have —" Before Stefan could finish Em put her finger on his lips for a moment and he stopped. As she gazed at him Stefan felt a wave of peace run through him, as if she knew what was coming and wanted him to take a moment to clear his mind. She pulled her finger away and traced it along his jawline. He closed his eyes and felt the tenderness behind the caress. Then he felt her lips press to his and he gathered her in his arms and carried her to the bedroom.

Chapter Nineteen

T he next morning Alisa, Sarah and Tommy arrived simultaneously at nine o'clock, so coffee, tea and bacon rolls were the order of the day before they got around to discussing the previous evening's activities. Stefan had already left at eight o'clock that morning with a rushed kiss and a promise to tell all upon his return.

Em smiled into her coffee. The passion of making love so long into the morning left her feeling satiated and slightly sleepy, so one hot shower and three coffees later she felt fit to face the day.

"Right ladies and gentlemen, what is on the agenda?"

"Chess!" cried Tommy.

Em eye'd Alisa and Sarah.

Alisa voiced her opinion. "You play while we look through the box, and if we find anything interesting you'll be ready and at hand to explain. How's that?"

"Yes!" said Tommy, happy to have a semblance of normal life with Em back.

The chess table was set by the front window, and the table pulled into the centre between the two sofa's, the paperwork was spread out to be organised.

An hour later Em said, "Ok Tommy, I think this is a good stopping place. What chores do you have to do today?" He rhymed off several items ending with bringing items from the coffee store to Em.

Remembering who Tommy had seen there, Em asked, "Tommy, do you think that you could maybe find out who the lady was that was at the coffee shop with Derek? Don't ask directly just kind of..." She searched for a way to explain.

"I know, I know, I'm good at finding things out," Tommy said pushing out his thin chest.

Em smiled and reached out to tousle his ginger hair.

"What do you want to know? You know how I can find out?" He continued in his hurried way of talking, "One of the girls that work there is the daughter, and she's in my class at school. She brings in cookies and stuff sometimes and she talks to me, she's kinda weird but nice."

Tommy stopped and looked at Em.

Used to his rapid conversations she had kept track of where he had left off.

"Tommy, I want to know who the lady is and how she knows Derek. Can you find out? And it's like a secret, so we don't want them to know why."

"Sure, no problem," said Tommy. "I'll see you later," and grabbing his coat headed for the door whistling, a recent trait since Tommy hadn't whistled a month before.

"Well, now that Tommy has his assignment, how have you ladies made out with yours?"

Sarah was in the kitchen working on sandwiches for lunch and peeked her head out. "Alisa, don't say a word till I'm there, I'll be done in two minutes with a luscious lunch."

Alisa winked at Em and began loudly, "Well let me tell you..." and then stopped as Sarah appeared again in the doorway, this time holding a knife still caked with the tuna fish from the sandwich she was cutting. She waggled it back and forth. "Don't make me come in there," before she realized how she looked and started laughing too.

A short time later the sandwich pile had dwindled, the crisps had disappeared and the only remains were the dregs of coffee and crumbs of the brownies.

There were several neat piles, a diary, notebook, research notes and other notes that looked like they were written in code.

"Anything interesting in the diary?" Em asked as she picked it up to look at it and then stopped for a moment as she stared at the handwriting she had not seen in three years. Her heart skipped a beat, pounded for a moment and then calmed down. Flipping quickly, she went to the page of the week that Peter died. Notes about things to do before they left for Scotland and a few meetings, one with Dean Simon two days before he died, a note about going to open a safety deposit box, and the day he died a large D with a question mark beside it, and no specific time.

"Do you think this means Derek? And why were they meeting?" Em asked, absently but aloud.

"Remember Derek said that he had met Peter a couple of times and that Peter was going to introduce you two, and that he was seen the day of the explosion? But it makes no sense that he would be involved, why would he do that?" asked Sarah. "And did it have to do with Peter's research? I mean Peter would never talk about it to me."

"Not much with me either," said Em. "His research had two areas and one he shared, working with safety manufacturers on explosives, and there was another avenue that he just would not talk about and I just left him alone with that because it made him happier. I wonder how we can find out?"

Alisa piped up. "I wonder what's in the safety deposit box?" Then picking through the papers she found a bank statement. "Wherever it is it's definitely paid for, this account's still open and it automatically pays for the box out of an account each year."

"But where's the key?" asked Sarah, as all three looked at the Chinese puzzle box, and in unison said: "He wouldn't."

"Oh yes he would," Em said. "If he wanted to keep something safe he would have several layers to it. Question is how do we open it?"

"Hammer?" suggested Sarah, known for her lack of patience.

"I wonder," said Em, lifting the box and examining it from all angles. There was no easy way to open it and not wanting to destroy the box, she put it on the table again.

Going to the trunk that now resided in the corner of the room, Em emptied the photos on the floor to reveal the bottom. The inside of the trunk was lined with red silk that appeared new compared to the ancient trunk. Taking scissors, she cut next to the seam, running along the side and pulled it back to reveal a flat wooden surface fitted into the bottom. Alisa wheeled over and Sarah stood behind her as Em examined it closely, seeing that it was inlaid in a similar design to the Chinese puzzle box.

"I don't believe this," whispered Em, cradling back on her heels to think. "There's got to be a way to open this." She leaned forward again and pulled all of the silk out of the trunk and bent to run her fingers over the surface, it was smooth at first touch, but as she continued she felt the small differences between the design in the woods.

"Maybe if you play the music it will open? Like using a magic password," suggested Alisa.

Em looked up puzzled. "What?"

"Look Em, its musical notes. They're kind of intertwined, but when you look down on it you can see it."

Looking back at the design, Em realised this was true, the intricate patterns revealed musical notes.

"Lovely, now can't we just say 'open sesame' or something?" declared Sarah, her frustration growing.

"Wait a minute," Em said as it dawned on her. "Alisa, what are the notes? Do you recognise the melody of the song?"

Alisa leaned over in her chair, examined the notes and started to hum, then smiling, she starting singing, "*Michèle, my belle _____*"

Em grinning from ear to ear jumped up and hugged Alisa. "You're a genius!"

"But how does that help?"

"I don't know why I didn't think of it before," said Em. "About six months after we met Peter gave me a Chinese puzzle box, and in the design, it spelled my name, and it was the pressure points you pushed to open the box, but it had to be in the correct order, so you had to figure out the name and then use that to open the box. Peter said that he always used names but used them in different codes."

"And Michèle was my aunt's name," said Sarah.

"Yes, it makes perfect sense that he would use a relative's name."

Using the letters M I C H E L E Em pressed the code into the notes in the box and a small door opened, dropping a safety deposit key into her lap.

At that moment Stefan opened the door to find Sarah, Em and Alisa laughing, crying and hugging.

"Do I even want to know?"

"Probably," said Em, "but you don't get to know just yet. You're not the only one who can keep a secret," she said, pocketing the key into her jeans.

Chapter Twenty

*T*ommy stared at the cakes in the display case and moved his eyes toward the door to the kitchen. Victoria sometimes went in to help on the weekend, but he wasn't sure if she was there.

"Hi Tommy," said Mrs. Columbo, the owner of The Coffee Bar, a busy cafe on the east end of Great Western Road and not far from Em's flat. "What can I get for you today?"

He hesitated and placed his coffee orders for his deliveries. It was such a good way to make money. He loved to buy surprises for his little sister, and he didn't want to ask his mother and father for the money as so much went to her specialised care, so he earned it by running errands for the people on Roberts Street. It was perfect, close to home, and he liked all the people he worked for, but especially Em. She was always so sweet and nice to him, no matter what, and she always encouraged him with his studies when he had trouble, especially with maths.

"Is that all Tommy?" Mrs. Columbo asked as she placed the bagged items on the counter.

"Yes," he answered, drawing the word out as he figured out whether to have a doughnut to delay his time or — the decision was made for him.

"Would you like to try a new doughnut?" asked Mrs. Columbo.

"Oh, yes please."

"Victoria!" she shouted toward the back, "would you bring out a fresh sugar cinnamon doughnut for Tommy please?"

Victoria appeared at the door. Tiny for her eleven years, she had long dark hair, eyes the colour of melted chocolate and clear beautiful skin. She smiled shyly.

"You have one too, honey, you've been working for a while, take a break," said Mrs. Columbo.

Tommy couldn't believe his luck, he could talk to Victoria without having to figure out a reason and he had a doughnut.

Mrs. Columbo arrived at the small corner table with two glasses of milk and two doughnuts, and left them alone as she assisted a customer. This was his favourite seat in the small cafe as you could see all the other tables and out the large front windows, revealing the busy walking traffic, and even busier road traffic.

"I can only sit while it's quiet," said Victoria. Small though she was, no one ever called her anything but Victoria.

"Okay," agreed Tommy.

Victoria pulled a small part from the doughnut and popped it into her mouth, following it with a sip of milk. She returned his gaze for a moment and then asked, "How is the studying going for the exams?"

"Oh, fine. What about you?" he asked, already knowing the answer as Victoria was one of the smartest girls in the class.

"I'm still working on it."

"Okay," said Tommy, struggling to find a way to bring up the topic of Derek and the mystery girl.

"Do you know lots of your customers?" he asked.

"Oh, a few. Aunt Vicki knows just about everyone that comes in, and that's quite a lot of people," she stated proudly.

"You know," Tommy said, finally striking on an idea, "there was a man here a short time ago, and I thought that he was in the football club, and then you know what happened, he was the man that was killed in the hit-and-run accident about a week ago. Did you know him?" As usual, the words came out in a rush.

Victoria was chewing her second bite and after another sip of milk, said thoughtfully, "Oh, I remember him. He's been in a few times, he tried to talk to Aunt Vicki about family in Italy, but she never seemed to say much about it. How do you know him again?"

Tommy warmed to the subject. "Well, when I saw him he looked just like the guy that plays for our local team and I was thinking that maybe I might get to visit the team or something…" he faded off as he saw her watching him closely. She had a way of doing that to people, just watching.

"You can't now anyway."

"Can't what?"

"Can't get to visit the team. You boys and your sports."

"It's sad though, do you think he has family or anything?" he asked, hiding behind his glass before taking a gulp of milk.

"I don't know, there was a woman with him once, kind of scary. She was pretty small and skinny, and everything she wore was black, black shoes, black sweater, black jeans, and a black hat, except her face was very white, and even then she had black hair and black eyes." Victoria shivered in her chair. "She was really skinny."

"Maybe she was his sister?"

"Oh no, I don't think so. She didn't look anything like him."

"Well that's not always so, I don't look anything like my sister. She's pretty and blonde and she has cool green eyes. So you don't have to look like them to be brother and sister," Tommy rambled on.

"Well, I don't think so. It was more than the looks, it was the way they talked."

"Like boyfriend and girlfriend?"

"Not really. Boy, what is your fascination with these two anyway?"

"Nothing, I just don't know anyone that's been killed by a car, and it's sad, and you know if he had a family it would be sad for them, and then what would they do? Would they come back here?"

"Tommy how you do ramble on about stuff." Victoria glanced up as the door opened with new customers arriving. "Back in a minute."

Tommy watched as she quickly put on her apron and smiled up at the customers. He was amazed how much her face changed when she smiled. He was struck by how pretty she was, he usually didn't pay much attention to girls, but when Victoria smiled she kind of, well, glowed.

Tommy felt the blush that matched his red hair, and hurriedly finished his doughnut and milk. He thought it best to wait at the table until she returned, which took just a few minutes.

She took off the apron, sat down, and noticing he was finished, proceeded to finish her own.

"Will you be here tomorrow?" Tommy asked.

"I think so, depends on my studies."

"Okay. Well, maybe if you're finished and you're here then maybe we could, I mean we could have another doughnut or something…" Tommy felt his face flush again and wished a hole would open up beneath his feet.

Victoria smiled and nodded, and Tommy grabbed his packages and left.

Alisa's phone rang and her eyes lit up, recognizing the ring. "Hello my love," the usual greeting.

She nodded and smiled and kept nodding as she listened. "Okay then, see you in an hour or so." She wheeled around. "I'm in the mood for a celebration!" she said. "Where shall we —" She caught herself, quickly changing it to, "What shall we do?"

"You guys go out, you all need a break," said Em.

No's sang in unison.

"I don't want to hold you back just because —" Em began and couldn't finish. It was the first time she had come face to face with the fact that she was holding her friends back from their lives and what they wanted to do because she couldn't go out into the world. She knew that it wasn't really that she was afraid of the world, it was that she was afraid of how she would react to it. She had been in the flat for three years until the explosion, and although she was out of her home, Stefan's was just across the hall and was beginning to feel like an extension of her own.

Em dropped to the sofa, and put her head in her hands.

Alisa wheeled over to her. "I'm so, so sorry Em, I didn't think. You know we don't have to go out." Em raised her head to look at her dear friend and felt a weight on her heart.

"No Alisa, I'm sorry. You were so happy just a moment ago and here I've gone and spoiled it for you. What's wrong with me? I mean I know what's wrong with me, but why can't I just make up my mind to go out? I don't think I'm weak —"

"No Em, you are not weak!" Alisa interrupted. "You went through so much when you lost Peter and the baby. We all have different ways of dealing with the problems and issues in life and sometimes we just need a break to deal with it. You are going to get better and you are going to be able to go out again. I know it — because I know you."

A single tear escaped Em's eye and trailed down her face.

"Remember Em," Alisa continued, "when I had the accident and you came to the hospital, and how supportive and loving and caring you were? And how strong you were to help me?"

"Grayson was there too," Em whispered.

"Of course he was, you both were, and if it wasn't for the both of you I don't know where I would be. Maybe I can't walk right now, but I love my life, my husband, and you my dear friend. Remember you said not to give up hope, well I haven't and although I may or may not ever walk again, I have hope about the possibility, and if there is one, Grayson and you will be there for me. So don't ever say that you are weak because you are the strongest woman I know."

Em's watery smile brightened her face and she leaned across and kissed her friend's cheek. "Guess I've been told then," she whispered.

"Well, I know what we're going to do," Stefan announced. "What's the number of that *Dinner at Eight* guy, Douglas? Let's get him around here and we'll have a feast."

Em looked around and marvelled at her luck in life to have such kind and loving people care about her.

Standing up smiling she said, "But what shall I wear?" Alisa and Sarah laughed and began speaking at the same time about what to wear.

Stefan shrugged his shoulders and went in search of a beer, and soon all the arrangements were made for a celebration feast to arrive at the flat that evening to be ready for eight o'clock.

Grayson arrived and was sent out again immediately with Sarah in tow round to her flat to bring a change of clothes, jewellery and all the sundry items associated with making a woman beautiful.

A crisp white wine served, Alisa and Em lounged on the sofas discussing the day's find. Stefan had since disappeared to shower, change and call to find out how John was feeling.

"What bank do you think he used?" asked Alisa, as she savoured the fruity wine. "And where would he have opened it?"

Pulling out her laptop she searched all the banks within five miles of the University.

"I don't think he would have used a bank that we had accounts at if he was trying to conceal something," Em said, which helped narrow the branches. Satellite office and banks that were not large enough to have deposit boxes were also eliminated. It still left twenty.

Alisa examined the key and could find no distinguishing marks. "Even if we figure out which bank it is, how do we get into it?" she asked. "We need a man and one who can sign like

Peter. For all they know, since the payments have continued Peter is still alive."

"One thing at a time," replied Em.

At that moment Grayson and Sarah arrived and soon afterwards corks were popped and champagne consumed as the women dressed for dinner.

"What are we celebrating anyway?" Grayson asked.

"I'm not sure," Stefan answered. "But as long as their happy, I'm content."

Grayson smiled at Stefan and raised his glass, "To happy wives and girlfriends."

୧୨

The previous night's activities had gone well and she had the money. Her plan had died with Derek, so she had to formulate a new plan.

What to do? She poured a whiskey and downed it, wincing at the flavour. God, it was awful stuff, but it was warm going down.

Opening the fridge she saw weeks old dry cheese, spoiled milk and eggs that were so old they would probably bounce off the water never mind float.

Pulling on the black coat she went to the Chinese takeaway on the corner. The food tasted like sawdust, but that was mainly the effects of the medication and she had to eat to keep going. Never mind, she could hang on another week or so and then it would all be over. And she would have revenge, for her father.

୧୨

It was midnight and much wine, food and bubbly had been consumed. Em stood at the window looking out at the intersection she had seen so many times, and while it had always brought comfort to her before, it now seemed strange and almost alien to her. The lights cast a muted yellow glow, and since it was the first snow of the new year there were fewer people out on the street.

Em started suddenly and focused more closely. Stefan stepped behind her and looked out over her head, even in high heels the top of her head barely touched his chin.

"What's out there that's so fascinating?"

"I'm not sure. I thought I saw a shadow move."

"Yes?"

"A small black shadow, like someone watching us." Stefan focused his eyes but couldn't see anything. He looked just to the right of the intersection and saw the van that he had requested be posted outside the flat.

He didn't want to draw attention by waving, so he continued to stare at the corner Em had pointed to, hoping they would get the idea and investigate, but he doubted it. When it came to surveillance it was too easy to get wrapped up in the wrong direction.

Pulling Em back Stefan went to close the drapes. "No please, not yet," Em said. "It's so beautiful with the snow falling."

"Then come back and view it from a distance."

"Stefan is it alright if I leave the chair here?" Grayson asked, pointing to Alisa's wheelchair. "I gather we'll be back tomorrow."

"No problem, but won't you need it?"

"No, I had the extra one dropped off at the hotel. Sorry Sarah," Grayson said to the pouting girl, "I need some alone time with my wife."

Sarah rolled her eyes. "You two think you're newlyweds!"

"We are," said Alisa as she put her arms around her husband's neck as he lifted her. "We've only been married for nineteen years out of the seventy we're expecting, that's like newlywed status."

With goodbyes said, Stefan turned to Em. "Would you like a nightcap before you retire, m'lady?"

"I would love that. Are you very tired?" Em asked

"Not really, why?"

"I wanted to talk a little."

They settled down with a whisky and a port. "Perfect time for a chat," Stefan said.

Chapter Twenty-One

M oira turned and looked at the clock, three o'clock in the morning. Why did she always wake up at three? Turning, she pulled up the covers and wished for retirement. At sixty she felt old and tired, even though she was efficient and never missed a day of work. Mike had died and left her penniless five years ago, and it had taken the past five years to build a small nest egg. She had that steely determination that saw her through lots of tough times, but although her will was as strong as ever, her body was getting older.

She had information that could be valuable, it had no monetary value to the police, and she thought it would never be worth anything. But ever since Alisa Grayson and Sarah Livingstone had shown up at the University she had to reconsider and so she had given them the box.

It would whet their appetite and then she could.... that was the question how should she do it?

She turned and looked at the clock again. Half an hour had passed.

Getting up, she took six steps from the tiny bedroom to get to the kitchen and boil some milk. As she stirred the milk in the pan, she considered her options.

I'll just have to wait for the moment, she told herself. *I'll just have to wait.* And since she had spent so much of her life waiting, waiting to marry, waiting for children, waiting for Mike to make his fortune, she was very practised at waiting.

So much for sleeping in the extra bedroom, Em thought as she turned and spooned into the curve Stefan made. He was warm and his soft breathing was a comfort to her. It was so nice because he didn't snore. Peter snored, but that was about the only thing he did that wasn't perfect.

Oh, what am I going to do? she asked herself. *I've come to care so deeply for Stefan in such a short time, and he was a mystery, less so now, but still.*

The talk had gone well, he had spoken of life after the death of his mother and how his father had died in the hospital shortly afterward, the drink had finally killed him, but Stefan thought it was more of a broken heart than any physical problem. He spoke of how he had gone into the military and had always provided for his younger sister. She now understood why she had never seen his sister. How he had gone into investigating and worked for the government and still did sometimes, and that's how he had the connections to have the explosives investigated by the likes of John and Will.

So much had happened in such a short time. Alisa coming back into her life, Derek, the long-lost brother that Peter had never mentioned to her. *Why not?* she wondered. They had shared everything, or so she thought, she began to consider what had they not shared. Other than his brother and some of his research, was there anything else he had kept from her? She couldn't imagine, but she knew one thing: she had to find out why he died, if Derek's death was related, and if it was, did it have anything to do with the explosion in her flat?

It was at that moment that it hit home with her. The certainty that the three had to be related. *Was someone after her? But why? What could she possibly know or have done that would cause someone to try and kill her?*

Her head was full of thoughts and they whirled around until they eventually quieted down and she drifted off to sleep, enough time to think of it tomorrow, and Stefan would be there to help. Dear, sweet, wonderful Stefan.

"What do you mean there's nothing left?"

"Just what I said, there's nothing left."

Stefan gripped the phone and counted to five. "Why not? Isn't there some molecular level or something microscopic?" he asked.

"Sure there is, but it isn't anything unusual, nothing to tie them together. At least at the moment," James answered. "Will says he wants to go back in, John does too."

"Why?"

"Well, they think it's a new formula, and you know what they're both like."

Stefan knew when it came to explosives that it was their passion, and a new type would be like catnip to a kitten. Stefan smiled as he reconsidered his analogy since neither would be considered anything like a kitten.

"I was afraid you were going to quarantine the entire block."

"I was going to," James answered, "but according to Will and John whatever is left is negligible and there won't be any more fireworks."

"Okay. So what do we know so far?"

"Well…" There was silence on the phone as James ruffled through some papers and came back tutting again.

Stefan listened for a few minutes. "Let me know what I can do. And when will they be coming back?"

"Okay," he answered tutting again as he hung up.

Em raised an eyebrow. Curled up on his chair, wearing his oversized shirt and with her curly blonde hair piled on top of her head, she looked young, vulnerable, and very sexy.

He shook his head to clear it and answer her unasked question.

"Yes, they are going to try to get more samples. Apparently, they think it's stabilised and they can't wait to find out more about it, so they'll be back later today, they're running tests on what's left of their case."

"Okay, what do I need to do?" Em asked.

Stefan squatted down in front of her and took her hands.

"We need to find out what type of explosive killed Peter. I have some contacts but it may take a while. Do you know anyone in California who can help?"

"No."

Stefan frowned.

"That's because Grayson and Alisa are here at the moment, not in California."

Stefan pinched Em and she squealed.

"Grayson is well…comfortable."

"Comfortable?"

"If you call having a few hundred million comfortable."

"Oh."

"So I think he might have some contacts," said Em. "I just wonder when they're going back."

"Why don't you call?"

"I will but it's still too early."

"It's ten o'clock!"

"Yes, but they were up late last night and we do have to give them some alone time."

"Alone time? They've been married for twenty years!"

Em smiled. "Yes, they have been happily married for almost twenty years, and that's how it stays happy. Anyway," she said, pulling Stefan closer and brushing her lips with his. "How would you like some alone time?"

John and Will parked the car and pulled a new sample case out of the trunk.

"Will you try not to either blow me to pieces or flatten me this time Will?"

"We'll see John," Will grinned at his partner.

John stubbed out the cigarette and coughed into his good hand as they headed up the stairs.

෨෩

She watched as they locked the car and left.

They didn't notice her, people rarely did. Like a chameleon she fitted into her surroundings. She always melted into the scene. Dammit, who called these guys in anyway? She'd heard about them, real geeks. They had almost caught her father about seven years ago.

She twisted the bright red locks of the wig around her finger as she thought, maybe this wasn't so bad after all. After a few more minutes she left the front step and wandered over toward the plain sedan they had parked. Bending to tie a shoelace she slipped a GPS tracker under the car, stood up and strolled down toward the infamous intersection. She loved tech.

CB80

"Alisa please hold onto the key and as soon as I figure out which bank it is, we'll also figure out how to get into the box."

"Okay," replied Alisa.The afternoon sun was low and it had started snowing again. "What else do we need to do?"

"Is there any way that you can get a report on the accident? Like a police report? Did the university do any investigation? I know you talked to Dean Simon, but he sounded like it wasn't much of an investigation. Wouldn't they have known the materials that were kept in the lab? Stefan says they need it for a comparison."

"Does he think it's related?"

"It's too much of a coincidence not to be. Peter dying, then Derek being killed, and then my flat being blown up."

"I know. Well, we're going to leave in the morning."

Grayson clicked off his phone. "We'll have more information in a few days. I talked to Greg Morrison and he's going to do some checking into the investigation, he's got a few friends on the force and he may just be able to get his hands on what we need."

"Can you email it to me?" asked Stefan.

"Yes, I will. What I'll do is leave my extra laptop here, it has an encryption software on it so when I send the information it will automatically be able to decrypt it for you."

The two men went to the office in the back to work on the details.

Em and Alisa looked at each other. "Glad they're getting along," said Alisa.

"Me too."

A knock on the door announced John and Will.

"Mrs. Lawson, can you please tell Stefan we have the sample we need and we're leaving now."

"Sure, and thank you very much." She looked at John's hand. "Does it hurt much?"

He lifted it and wiggled his fingers. "No problem," he said. "I can still smoke a cigarette."

Em wrinkled her nose. "As long as it's okay."

"I've had much worse, but thanks for asking."

CR&O

Looking at the laptop screen she sipped the whiskey.

I never thought it would be in that part of town, she said to herself. What an added bonus, trouble for that nosey team as well as getting rid of the witch.

She leaned back and rubbed her spine side to side against the corner edge of the wall. It would add a few days to the timeframe but no matter, she had the time, the new drugs were helping with the pain.

She rubbed her eyes. She needed sleep, it had been about two days and she was beat.

Heading to bed, she pondered the source of her materials. Money was no worry, she wanted the best quality.

Crawling under the warm duvet she fell asleep dreaming of red flames and death.

CR&O

"Yes, I can hear you Alisa, don't shout," Em said.

"Sorry about that, I think we hit some turbulence. Anyway, as I was saying, I got a call from Moira, remember, from Dean Simon's office? She says that she's come across some additional information we may be interested in."

"What do you think it might be?"

"I'm not sure, but I think it may be about the day of the explosion, she was the one who supplied the original box of investigation materials, and don't forget she remembered about the locker when it was convenient timing, which gave us the Chinese box and other information. To be honest I think she's holding something back, but don't worry, as soon as I've seen her, I'll call and fill you in."

At Grayson's waving Alisa ended the call with, "I've got to go, turbulence is getting a bit wild."

Chapter Twenty-Two

*M*oira hung up the phone. *Well, I've done it now*, she thought. She immediately picked the phone back up and made the reservation, then headed into the bedroom and surveyed the mess. *That's it, most of it goes, actually, most of it stays.*

She ran a few quick errands and after a couple of hours her three cases were packed. Either way, she was done with this place and if it all worked out she would be headed south for a luxury little place in the middle of a small resort where she could live well on very little, in the sun with a warm beach.

She settled down to wait with a fashion magazine, a first in her life, and after years of waiting on Mike and waiting for all the other disappointments this was just a short blip.

"I don't like you going in on your own Alisa."

"Grayson, don't worry, you're waiting for me in the car, right? So I'll be a few feet away, and Moira's sixty if she's a day, she's hardly a threat."

Grayson dropped a kiss on his wife's forehead. "It doesn't matter how gentle or not they may be, it involves you and that is all that concerns me."

Alisa smiled and blushed. Even after all these years of marriage Grayson still acted like a protective new boyfriend at times. She touched the fingers that rested on her shoulder. "I'll have my phone right next to me," she said.

"Would you like a tea or coffee, Mrs. Drew?"

"Please call me Alisa, and thank you Moira, may I have a tea?"

"Certainly," said Moira and disappeared into the kitchen.

Alisa circled the small living room, taking in all the details of the bedroom, the turmoil and the packed cases. Back to where she started, she was flipping through the fashion magazine when Moira returned.

"I just love all the new looks in this magazine, do you prefer the styles in this month? They had some nice new colours in the last one though."

"Oh, I didn't see that one," said Moira. "I know I'm not quite as young as those people but..." she trailed off, knowing Alisa would understand.

"Yes, I understand," said Alisa, taking the offered tea.

Moira sipped her tea and looked at the open magazine on Alisa's lap. Alisa as always was perfectly attired, wearing a simple yet elegant red suit with a cream sweater.

Moira considered it and rightly assumed that it cost more than she made in a month. Yet, as she looked at Alisa she was not jealous, Alisa always evoked a gentle and warm response.

"Moira, let's be honest with each other," Alisa came to the point. "You have some information that may or may not be of help to the police, but is definitely of interest to me."

Moira looked at her steadily. "Yes."

Alisa picked up the magazine and pointed to a picture of a woman in a linen summer suit. "You know, I think that this would really suit you, but maybe in a light green rather than blue?"

Moira looked at the picture and agreed.

Changing the subject Alisa asked, "How long have you worked for Dean Simon?"

Moira considered for a moment. "About fifteen years."

"That's quite a while."

"We have a good working relationship."

"That means you have quite a bit of patience."

Moira smiled. "I suppose so."

"When do you expect to retire?"

"When I'm a hundred," Moira said wryly.

"How much will it take to retire now?"

"Not too much."

"Don't undersell yourself Moira." Alisa waited a moment, then staring at Moira continued. "I think that you should retire earlier."

"Thank you, Mrs. Drew."

"Please, call me Alisa." she repeated.

Moira looked at Alisa and nodded.

Moira settled back into the worn covered chair. "You know that Peter was quite a coup for the University, with his reputation and then his research. Not to mention the donations that rolled in with his presentations. So they were anxious to entice him to stay, they were watching him closely. I liked him. He had a quiet, sincere way that was very endearing, and then there was a subtle change when he met Emily. He became more content with life and was quite irresistible with that beautiful smile." Moira's face softened at the memory before she continued.

"In the weeks when he was getting ready to leave anyone could see he was still happy, but there was something else. He was very distracted and worried about something. The day of the explosion I remember that the weather was lovely. It was spring and that Sunday the time changed forward one hour. I always change mine the night before as a rule, so that when I wake up in the morning I don't have the nasty surprise that I have lost an hour. Anyway, I had to stop by the office for some papers for the Dean. I took the bus in the early afternoon and was walking in by way of the old parking lot, it takes you by Peter's lab. I remember the sky was so blue and I was thinking that I would plant my garden that week, it had been cool before then —" Moira broke from her reverie. "Sorry, when one get's to remembering!"

"No it's okay, please go on," said Alisa.

133

"Would you care for a wine instead?" Moira asked.

"Actually, that would be wonderful. And do you mind if I make a call?"

"No, the phone is right there."

"It's okay, I have my mobile." Alisa pressed the preset number. "Hiya."

"Hello love, are you okay?"

"Yes dear, and it's going just fine. Can you give me a while?"

"As long as you're okay."

"Promise. Can you give me an hour?"

"I'll be back in exactly one hour."

"Perfect love, see you then."

"Bye, now."

Moira returned with two glasses of white wine. "I'm not sure if it is what you're used to, but it seems very nice to me."

"Moira, I've had some lovely wines at five dollars and some horrific ones at a hundred dollars. If it tastes good, it's a lovely wine." Alisa sipped. "And this is just lovely," which was true. It was a fruity light California white wine, which she considered a favourite.

"So please Moira, continue."

"Well as I was saying, Peter was worried about something, I assumed it was all wrapped up with the leaving and such, so I was walking toward the office and Peter's lab was set back, surrounded by those lovely palm trees, anyway he seemed to be having a heated conversation with this tiny woman with long dark hair. He was animated and quite distracted and she seemed quite angry about something. He walked into the building and she followed more slowly, so she was still in the lobby area, and then there was the explosion. I started to run to the building, but before I got very far I saw this woman helping Peter out of the front door of the building."

Alisa looked up sharply.

"Yes, Peter. Well I was about to run over to help, and she was pulling him along a certain way, and then I looked more closely

134

at him and he was dressed in completely different clothes than Peter, he had on a t-shirt and jeans and Peter was wearing a white collared shirt and khakis with loafers."

Before Alisa had a chance to question, Moira continued. "Why would he change his clothes? He had been in the building just long enough to put the codes into the lab before it blew up. Not unless he was a quick-change artist. And there was one more thing. The man she helped away, as well as the change of clothes, he had slightly longer hair, and it was in a small ponytail at the back of his head, that was the only difference when you looked at his face you'd swear it was Peter."

"Why didn't you tell the police?"

"What was I to tell them? I saw Peter? Or the twin of Peter being led out of the building? No one else saw him and there wasn't any other evidence that he was there. But he is the one who knows something, talk to him and you'll find out about the explosion."

Yes, we would, Alisa thought, *if he wasn't dead too.*

"Why is this worth a retirement?" Alisa asked.

"Because the University would have to explain that there was someone else there and that it might not have been an accident as they were so fond of holding on to. I may only feel it, but those two had something to do with the explosion and his death and since Peter died in the explosion it couldn't have been a complete accident, the way it was portrayed. My information is no use to the police and it may have been some use to Mrs. Lawson if she wanted to investigate, but she left. I know it may seem like something small, but I can prove that someone was there at the time of the explosion, Peter's doppelgänger, as well as a woman."

Moira leaned back in the chair and sipped her wine.

Alisa considered for a moment. It wasn't a lot, but it would be from the University standpoint. It would reopen the investigation that they had worked so hard to close and it would prove that there was someone there, innocent or not, at the time of the explosion.

"Moira, I feel that there may be more, and while I am happy to contribute to your retirement, I feel —"

"There's one more thing," Moira interrupted. "I know who the girl was."

Alisa waited.

"I saw a picture once with Peter and the girl, along with an older man, her father I think. I did a little research and found out that there was an explosion at the University Peter attended, and it involved the old man in the picture. Some students died and he was sent to prison for the accidental deaths."

"I see," said Alisa.

"Do you? It may be supposition but it definitely was weird, and I know the University didn't want anything to get out, so I just forgot about what I saw, then when it was put up as an accident, what else could I prove? I've never seen either him or her from that day to this."

"Moira," said Alisa, "I think that the linen suit should definitely be part of your retirement plan." At that moment her phone buzzed, and she answered. "Yes dear, I'm just finishing. By the way, I'd like to open a new account at the bank. Raising her eyebrows Alisa looked at Moira and asked what she thought about the beginning balance.

Moira agreed and went to put the final items into her overnight bag.

"No, I haven't heard anything yet Sarah. Alisa said she would call as soon as she knew something."

"I knew that I should have gone with them," Sarah said, impatient for news.

"Why didn't you? You could have done some work on the paintings."

"Yes, I know, I just don't want to leave yet, I have a funny feeling."

"You just don't want to miss me," said Em, smiling and refilling Sarah's wine glass.

Sarah agreed and sipped the wine. A moment later Em's phone rang. It was Alisa.

During the conversation with Alisa the street buzzer rang and a minute later Detective Inspector Ian Roberts and Detective Constable Laura Miller came into the lounge.

Sarah took them into the kitchen to make tea and give Em time to finish the conversation with Alisa.

A few minutes later there was a knock on the front door and there stood Tommy with the Friday afternoon delivery.

He trailed Sarah into the kitchen. "Where's Em?" he asked. "I found out something, not very much, but I did find out something and hopefully—" his voice died away as he saw the strangers in the kitchen.

His face once again reflected the red of his hair and he stood there with his hands behind his back, rocking back and forth on this heels.

"Hello," said the DS and DC in unison.

"Hello," replied Tommy, who visibly relaxed when Em entered the kitchen behind him and placed her hands on his shoulders.

"Thank you for the messages, Tommy. Shall we play our game of chess in the morning?"

He nodded, turned and smiled up at her before flying out the door. He wasn't sure what was going on, but there were way too many adults around for him to be comfortable.

"You seem to have him wrapped around your little finger," observed DC Miller.

"He's a sweet boy and is always so reliable with his errands, that's how he makes his little living, and I've just introduced him to chess, which he is remarkably good at now."

Sarah chimed in. "Shall we have the tea here or in the lounge?"

"I think this is quite comfortable for the moment," said DS Roberts, and they settled into the tall chairs around the island table in the kitchen.

"We just wanted to stop by to inquire if you have thought of anything else about Derek Lawson we should know about, and to ask if you thought it may have anything to do with the explosion in your flat? Also, we're very glad to see you safe and sound."

Em blew on her tea before sipping and thought for a moment. "Do you think there may be a connection?"

DC Miller answered, "it is certainly a strange coincidence."

"I have lived here, well in my flat, quietly for three years and then all this starts to happen, I don't know what caused it. Really, all I know is that he wanted to speak to me about Peter and we had one visit and he was killed shortly after, I don't know why."

"Do you know why you're under surveillance?" DS Roberts asked.

"What!?" exclaimed Sarah, sitting up straight and putting the cup down with a bang.

"Why is someone watching this building, this flat?" Detective Roberts asked.

"I think that that would be an excellent question for Stefan, he owns this place, not me. I'm just staying for a while until mine is repaired."

"Not to be too nosey ma'am, but why not go to a hotel?" asked Miller.

"I prefer to stay close to my own flat as some of my own things are still in it," Em said.

"But unusable…" prompted the police officer.

"I really just don't go out much and I just prefer it this way," stated Em in a firm tone. "Is there anything else?"

"Yes, just a couple of other things. Derek Lawson was seen with a small dark-haired woman a couple of times, do you know who she is?"

"Absolutely no idea," replied Em.

DS Roberts nodded. "What have you been told about the explosion?"

"Nothing really, there have been investigators here, but not a thing."

"And who do you think placed explosives in your bedroom and why?"

"Again, I have no idea. I just don't know."

"Do *you* have an idea?" Sarah asked DS Roberts.

"It is an ongoing investigation with no real suspects yet, Ms. Livingstone," was the non-committal reply.

Sarah leaned back in the chair and rubbed her temples, she hated answers that weren't answers.

"One more thing, Mrs. Lawson," detective Roberts said rising. "If you should hear anything about this woman who knew Derek Lawson, please do call us."

Handing over the card DC Miller said, "we are here to help Mrs. Lawson, please do call us."

"What about those people who are watching the flat?"

DS Roberts smiled at Em. "Oh, you nailed it on the head, talk to Mr Lundgren and you'll find out who they are."

"And what about the investigation into the explosion?" Em asked.

"Oh, we are in contact with that team and will be sharing information."

Sarah showed them out the door and returned to the lounge, where she found Em staring out the window from the side behind the curtain.

Sarah started for the window.

"Wait, Sarah," said Em.

Em waited for the Detective Sergeant and Detective Constable to leave and watched where they went. As they headed for the car parked across the street DS Roberts looked directly at Stefan's window and then at a workman's small lorry a few spaces down, then got into his own car.

Em watched the lorry for a few minutes, studying it for activity, seeing none she drew back from the window.

"I know that particular lorry hasn't been there every day, but he's right, now that I think of it there has been a lorry on that corner. That particular spot does have the best viewpoint of this flat."

Em sat on the sofa to think for a minute, then, looking a Sarah patted the seat next to her and Sarah sat and put her hands in her face. Em put her arm around her.

"What is it, Sarah?"

"What's going on Em? First Peter dies in an explosion, then Derek is killed, then you were almost blown up and now this place is being watched." Sarah rubbed her temples again. "What a good friend I am," she said. "I'm supposed to be helping you and here you are calm as anything."

"No sense getting worked up about it since we don't know what's going on, but I think we'll find out soon."

Em pulled out the phone and called Stefan. It went right to his voicemail and so she left a message for him to call, adding that the police had just been in on another visit.

Chapter Twenty-Three

❝When is Franco due to visit? You said you knew." asked James, tutting at the end of the sentence.

Stefan sat back in the chair with his feet crossed on the corner of the desk and watched as James steepled his hands.

"He'll be coming in a few night's time, just be patient. I've heard that they're on schedule for the visit."

"Why is he coming now?"

"His mistress is pregnant, and he's coming to deal with the situation."

"How did you find that out?" James asked

"Just a matter of knowing all the wrong people. Now, how is the crew doing with the surveillance on my flat? Anyone else watching it?"

"Not that we can see, just the normal residents. It is a bit tricky you know, there's a major intersection right there and all kinds of people walk up and down, we have good resources, but we can't investigate everyone who walks down the road."

"No, I don't need that, just anyone who seems to have an interest in our street."

"Don't worry," tutted James.

Stefan stood up and stretched, towering over James. "Oh, but I do worry, I do."

Em answered Stefan's call with "Stefan, we need to talk."

"Isn't that what we're doing?"

"Seriously."

"Okay, seriously."

"Not on the phone okay, this is serious. Yes it is Stefan."

"I have a few things to take care of, how about dinner at eight? I'll bring something home and make a nice quiet dinner and you can interrogate me, and I promise to answer all your questions, even the tough ones."

Content, Em hung up the phone and went to her computer. With all the uproar of activities, she hadn't even looked at work recently, so she busied herself with emails and viewed a few writing projects, trying to decide which was the most interesting. Research projects were fun but challenging when she had to work out how to view documents from home, but with the internet, most documents were now available to view online.

A few hours later she called Sarah to check on her.

"Oh, I'm fine, I've been working on some sketches, and I'll start one of the paintings in the morning. How about lunch tomorrow and we can catch up on things?"

"Sounds perfect," said Em.

"Oh, by the way, is the lorry still there?"

"Yes," said Em. "I just checked and it's still there."

"You sure they're not just doing work on the street?"

"Yes, I've only seen one guy go out and then back in again, workmen usually stay outside the lorry, not in it."

Sarah sighed. "When will Stefan be home?"

"About eight."

"I'll feel better when he is, at least I'll know your safe then."

"Don't worry little one, I'm fine."

Em hung up the phone and headed for a hot shower where she could think and reflect. One thing was sure though, Em couldn't believe how easily she had slipped into staying at Stefan's place, it was immaculate, beautifully designed yet homey and comfortable. Even more confusing were the emotions that she felt for Stefan, she was so at ease with him. Letting the hot water flow over her she began to imagine what it would be like going on a walk to the park, or down to the local pub, she had heard so much about, she loved the name, The Liquid Ship, with a pirate motif, and apparently there was a quiz every Thursday. Even better, a long walk on the beach. She missed little of her former life, but the things she missed most were the palm trees and walks on the beach and the sound of the ocean sending her to sleep.

She sighed, stepped out of the shower, and directly into the steely gaze of a small, scrawny, dark-haired woman. Em grabbed for the basin as she felt a wave of nausea and her knees turn rubbery.

"Don't worry, I'm leaving. I just had to see you up close for a minute. I'm quite disappointed, you don't go out and your knees turn to jelly just by looking at me. Oh, don't worry I haven't left anything on this visit, it wouldn't be detectable if I had, but I haven't."

And with that, the strange woman with the huge black eyes strolled to the front door and walked out.

Em slid to the floor her shaking hands covering her face. Who was this woman and what did she want? And more to the point how did she get into Stefan's flat?

"Some team you are, a skinny little drink of water just floats past you and into my flat and you don't even know about it!?" Stefan bellowed into the phone.

"What? You did what?" he continued his tone only slightly lower. "Well, that's better than, get it processed and get it up here so I can have a look."

Em curled up on the sofa with her fingers laced around a steaming hot cup of tea, looking at the card for Detective Roberts that appeared to be glaring at her from the table.

She dialled the number and left a message for him to come around the next day as she had information. A few minutes later her phone rang, it was DC Miller, confirming and asking what the information concerned.

"Nothing I can talk about now," Em answered, "but please come by tomorrow."

Stefan sat next to Em and patted her knee. "You have to eat something soon you know."

Em felt a physical knot in her stomach. "Okay, but I can't just yet."

"Alright, but you need something stronger than tea," he said, pouring her a small bourbon neat.

She gulped it down and curled more into the corner of the sofa.

"What about going to a hotel?" Stefan asked.

"No Stefan I can't. I mean I'm not ready yet, it would make everything so much worse."

"I just want to know how the hell she got in here."

"I don't know, I thought that I had locked the door," Em said.

Stefan raised his eyebrow. More than once he had found it unlocked when Em was home in his flat, as well as her own.

A few minutes later there was a knock on the door and two small wiry men in worker's clothes came into the front lounge with a memory stick. They plugged it into Stefan's laptop and a black and white picture came into view. It was of the front landing and the stairs between Stefan's flat and Em's. They watched the comings and goings of earlier in the day and then they saw the small dark figure walk out the door. All in black, hands in pockets of an oversized coat with an oversized floppy hat on, it was almost unidentifiable as a woman.

Em nodded. "That's her."

Detective Roberts stood with his hands clasped behind his back facing out the window. Turning he asked once again, "Do you have any idea how she got in?"

Em shrugged her shoulder's. "I don't know."

"Well we know it wasn't through the front door, so we need to find the rathole and cover it up."

"What are the chances of going to a hotel for a few days?"

Em shook her head and Stefan placed his hands on her shoulders. "DS Roberts, I know you're concerned, and so am I, but I'm not going to force Em to do anything."

"You know, something like this may be just the thing to get you out," DC Miller suggested.

Em shook her head. "It won't. I won't be forced into doing something just because someone is trying to scare me. She did momentarily, but I will not be dictated to. I'm staying - as long as it's okay with Stefan."

He squeezed her shoulders once more. "Em is staying as long as she wants and that's that," he stated.

"Your surveillance wasn't much help," observed DS Roberts.

"It wasn't all bad, I had several views but *may* have missed one perspective."

"Missed?" Roberts raised an eyebrow.

Stefan shifted and viewed Roberts. "One camera on the front door, yes, but it was the specific camera angled right outside Em's door that caught her."

"Well, I just wanted to ensure that all avenues were covered."

Em turned to look at Stefan. "You did this?"

"Yes, it seemed to make sense, to cover both doors and the entrance."

"Who she is and what she wants are the key questions," said Em.

"She's been involved from the start you say?" asked Roberts.

"Yes, she was seen with Derek in California just after the explosion that killed Peter."

"Too many coincidences."

"There is one other thing, she was seen with Derek here also." Em related the information that Tommy had given her from the time he saw her in the coffee shop, and Miller took note of the Coffee house information.

Excusing themselves, DS Roberts and DC Miller left.

"What do we do next?" asked Em.

"Lunch and a movie, you need to take your mind off things and we've not had time together lately. I need my Em fix," Stefan said.

From the kitchen, Stefan called James. "I need a set of plans for this building, and I need another set of cameras installed. I want this place hermetically sealed."

CRØD

She laughed as she thought about the look on Emily Lawson's face when she stepped out of the shower. Weak at the knees! Haha!

She poured another scotch, rubbed her left knuckle and switched the TV channel.

They would increase the surveillance around the flat, but that didn't matter, she would still be able to get in and out without anyone knowing. Peter had owned that flat for years and showed her all its little secrets.

She frowned. *I just don't get it*, she thought to herself. *What did he see in her? And Derek, and that little twit messenger boy?*

The phone vibrated and she answered. "I don't know what other jobs I'll be doing, I'll let you know."

Silence.

"I said I'd let you know," and she clicked end before they could irritate her further.

Pouring herself another drink she sipped as she considered the plan. Very simple, but effective. Her father had taught her to evaluate any and every viewpoint so a contingency would be in place. Of course, it didn't work for him when those two students did the unexpected. Best not to think about that, she would only get upset and that would ruin her concentration.

She clicked the channel again and set to watch some mindless drivel of a reality show.

The vibration of the phone woke her up.

Yes, she had the money. Where and when to meet? Okay, that was set. That was the final detail, one more week and it would be finished.

CXEO

They had talked long into the night and Stefan had told her all, and now as they lay snuggled under the warm duvet she thought about this man who was so good and kind and so very gentle to her. He had seen so much hurt and violence in his own life. She thought about Peter and how bright and energetic he was, yet there was a side of his life that she never knew. She loved him so much, and she always would, but she was starting to realise that he would never return to her, and she lived in the here and now. And here was a man who was going to such lengths to protect her. She felt him stir next to her and pull her closer to him.

"Why aren't you sleeping?"

"Just remembering a different life."

He was silent for a moment. "Do you wish that you were still in that life?" he asked.

"Part of me has longed for it, but I've changed in these last few weeks. I'll never know what that life would've brought me. But I know this. This life here" —she laid her hand on his cheek — "is a lovely life."

"Even though someone is trying to end it?"

"I wouldn't change it because of her. Whoever she is, she's brought us together. I don't know that this would have ever happened without all this mess. So yes, even though someone is trying to kill me I feel alive, and part of life in a new way."

Stefan brought her closer into his embrace and it was a long time before sleep came for either of them.

Chapter Twenty-Four

"Grayson, have you found out anything about Peter's death?" Alisa asked over breakfast.

The early morning haze of the ocean had burned off and the January day was warm and sunny. The balcony off of their bedroom suite was on the top level and you could see far on a lovely day.

Pouring coffee and offering him the last Danish, Alisa rolled her chair to face the ocean view.

"I am baffled," he went on to explain. "It seems all of the forensic evidence has evaporated off the planet. And whatever Peter was working on, he kept it to himself. He was in negotiations with the government about a new trace element for a new explosive but didn't provide them with any information on either. They were just about to bring him in for an official interview when he died. And he was leaving shortly after that. I've put a call into Barry," he said, naming a private investigator who had been a close friend since college. "What about the safety deposit key?"

"Well," said Alisa holding up the key, "I found out something interesting. While quite similar, all safety deposit keys are not the same, and this particular one belongs to a small local bank. I just need to find a volunteer to go to the bank and take out what's in the box."

"And who are you going to persuade to do that?"

"Not you."

"Smart move."

"I might have tried but you are too well known for being you, and you couldn't play someone else if your life depended on it. I was considering Al," she said.

"Al?"

The family chauffeur was a similar build to Peter although younger, and had quite a talent with drawing, something that Sarah was mentoring during her visits.

"Well, he has curly hair."

"But it's blond."

"Yes, but we have washed out hair dye and —"

"— and I don't want to know any more," Grayson said putting up his hand. "You just be very careful. As a matter of fact, just stay here when whatever goes on goes on."

"Alright," grumbled Alisa but with a smile. "You like to spoil all my fun."

"Just call me a spoilsport," he said and kissed her forehead before leaving.

"How about if I send Mary along with him?" Alisa asked as he was heading out the door.

"Anyone but you my love."

"Okay," Alisa agreed, trying to figure out a way to go without breaking her word. She shrugged her shoulders and went to call for Mary, but was pre-empted as Mary came through the door.

"I have the hair dye Alisa, what are we doing?"

Alisa explained the plan.

"Oh yes, Al will love it," said Mary. "I just hope that he doesn't get the wrong idea about this and starts a life of crime."

"Well, strictly speaking, Em, as Peter's wife, has a right to the box and she just isn't here, and Peter is dead so he really can't open it, suffice to say that we are merely obtaining something that belongs to Em anyway."

"Your logic never changes," observed Mary. "It always *sounds*, logical."

"Yes, but you've been listening to it for the last twenty-five years Mary, you could probably quote me on anything."

"Oh no," said the grey-haired woman. "You are decidedly your own woman. Now let's call this young man and set him on the task."

One hour later the curly blond hair was curly dark hair, and Al was dressed for the part. As an artist he also had an affinity for duplicating signatures and after a few tries had perfected the forgery.

Alisa was firm in her statement. "Al, we are doing this with Emily Lawson's permission, and there are extenuating circumstances. I am not saying that forging a signature is acceptable in the general sense."

Al grinned. "I know Mrs. D. You and my mom have drilled it into me. I may be good at it, but I don't need to make a living at it, you guys pay me too well."

Alisa smiled in return satisfied. Al was a good responsible young man and they did pay him generously, but he deserved it. He studied hard and worked on his art and he supported his mother, so the fact that he didn't do an excessive amount of driving did not bother Alisa at all.

"Please don't tell your mother, she may not let you work here anymore," Alisa said.

"Oh, don't worry about that Mrs. D. My mom thinks you're an angel," he said with a wink. "But it'll be our secret anyway."

"Okay you two, get going," Alisa said handing the key over. "And please call me the minute you get whatever is in the box."

"A what was in the safety deposit box?" laughed Em.

"You heard me," said Alisa, "one of those blasted Chinese puzzle boxes, with a different design on it, and it's not musical notes."

"Oh, this is too much. What kind of design?!

"Tell you what, I'll take a photo with my phone and send it to you now. I don't know what to do I don't want to wait but who knows what is inside? Grayson isn't here right now, I'll have to wait as he's in a building with no phone coverage."

The photo came through and Em considered the picture and then called Alisa back. "Can you get a closeup of the top of the box and all the sides and send them to me in a file attachment in an email?"

"Sure."

"I think I may know how to figure it out."

"How?"

"Let's wait till I see the photos then I'll let you know."

"Okay. By the way Em, how are you doing?"

"I'm fine. I have to say that Stefan has been wonderful."

"You do know that he's in love with you?"

Em was silent.

"Em, don't tell me you don't know! You'd have to be the only one, it's written all over his face."

I guess... I just don't want to think of that right now, I'll think of it later. Alisa?"

"Yes, Em?"

"I'm glad we're back in touch again. I've missed having you in my life."

Alisa smiled into the phone and it carried through in her tone. "Me too Em, me too."

"What do you think Stefan? What does your photographer's eye see?"

"It's a pattern, but not a chronological one."

Em leaned back in the office chair and smiled. "I think it's a code of some kind. There was one like this in a Sherlock Holmes mystery story, Peter was crazy for mysteries. Anyway, it was dancing men and each position of the dancing men stood for a letter. I think that this is just like that."

"Was Peter just paranoid or what?"

Em frowned. "No, he wasn't, but he was creative and if he wanted to hide something then he found a creative way to do it in plain sight, like the old adage, where everyone can see but no one notices."

151

"But his boxes are all hidden."

"In some cases, yes, but he gave me one the first year we were together and he had another that he kept silly things in. He loved puzzle boxes so it makes sense that he would also hide something of value in it and if you crushed the box then whatever was inside would be destroyed also. Very ingenious if you ask me."

"You are biased," observed Stefan.

"A bit, but I still think it's cool."

"You California people and cool."

Em smiled at the teasing, and she shook her head. "Now quit distracting me and let's get on with breaking this code."

After a few hours and many cups of coffee later, Em threw down the pen in impatience.

"I can't figure it out."

"Maybe we're trying too hard, let's be logical about this," said Stefan.

An hour later they had the code. ELIZABETH. That was his grandmother's name.

"But how do we open the box now?"

"We press the figures in the correct order that spell out the name Elizabeth."

"Hi Alisa, I think we've figured out how to open the box." Putting the phone on speaker Em went through the description and a minute later heard a squeal of joy.

"I've got it!"

"Drop me off at the station Laura and you head over to the coffee place and see what you can find out there. I'll get a line on that incident in California."

"What do you think about the situations at Lundgren's?"

"Oh, she's safe enough there, Lundgren won't let anything happen to her. He'll stay with her from now on and don't forget the team outside. Plus I'm sure since this last incident he'll have another team on it, don't forget the connections he's got."

Laura Miller glanced quickly. "How good are they?"

"Two-fold, the work he's done for the government plus the money he's got."

"Money?"

"Oh yes, he's worth a few million quid. He owns the building he lives in, except for the Lawson flat, as well as the building across the street."

"But it's not listed that way."

"Laura, I'm not without my own connections. Speaking of, how is your brother doing?"

It never failed to surprise Laura the little things that Ian would pick up on. "He's doing well, he's talking about going to the races next week."

"Oh?"

"Yes, he always talks about going to events, it's just he never does. Anyway, what are you going to do?"

"Me? Oh, I have to call in on an old colleague for a catch-up."

Laura looked at Ian, trying to decide if he was serious or teasing, as he sometimes did. But it would keep, she would find out later.

The two men shook hands.

"Good to see you again Ian."

"Yes, James."

"Can I offer you a coffee? Tea? Something else?"

"Tea please."

James rang for the secretary and asked for two teas.

After the minor pleasantries had passed Ian came to the point.

"I keep running into one of your men on my investigation, thought you might want to provide a little assistance?"

James leaned back and tutted through his fingers. "I, eh…"

"Let me narrow it down for you. I'm looking into the death of Derek Lawson, and the explosion at Emily Lawson's flat. It's right across from Stefan Lundgren, one of yours."

"He's not one of mine," James was quick to respond.

Ian sighed. "Let's make it theoretical then if he were one of yours..."

"Yes, then what?"

They were interrupted for the moment by the arrival of tea and scones, then continued.

"Does the explosion have anything to do with one of your investigations?" Ian asked.

"Absolutely not."

"Then why were two of your best men out at the flat looking around?"

James sighed and decided on the truth. "Stefan called and wanted them in to investigate, seems to me he has a thing for the young Mrs. Lawson, anyway he's come to her rescue."

"And he's not doing anything for you at the moment?"

"Nothing to do with the explosion."

"So he is working on something?"

"Well, yes, but only on the peripheral - more he's feeding us with information."

"And what did your boys find out?"

James rang the buzzer. "Miss Jones, will you please send in Will and John."

"Yes sir," replied the crisp voice.

A few minutes later the two experts showed up.

After introductions, James instructed them to tell what they knew.

John began. "Well, it's a new chemical and it can be set off in a few different ways, but one of the most interesting is water, it reacts just like nitroglycerin. We have to run a few more tests, but when we first ran a scan on the room we couldn't find any traces of a chemical remotely used as an explosive and there was no detonator in the room and no trace evidence of any incendiary device."

"In other words, it's an explosive that can't be traced," said Will.

Ian thought about that for a minute. "Wait a minute, you're saying that this is an explosive element which won't show up on any scanner or in any test?"

"Right," Will answered.

"But that means..."

"Yes, it's something new and extremely valuable, and we are looking into recent incidents to see if it's new on the market and if it is, then we have got a serious problem on our hands."

"An international problem," said Ian.

"Yes, it could be transported anywhere and not show up. And since it's not a liquid it won't be checked, and it's water that is component that activates it."

Ian whistled.

James leaned forward. "Now you see why we're as anxious to investigate as you are? And in this case, I'm of a belief that joining forces is a good idea."

"Well that's a first," Ian commented.

"So what do we do next?"

"Well I have an idea," Ian said and set forth to explain.

Chapter Twenty-Five

"Mrs. Russo, have you ever seen this man before," Detective Constable Laura Miller asked.

Mrs. Russo looked at the photo. "Yes, he's actually a distant cousin of my Aunt."

Vicky Russo looked at the tall slim policewoman. "He died in a car accident."

"Yes ma'am, and we're just tying up a few loose ends. Did he come in often?"

"Not really, he first came about three-and-a-half years ago and then was gone for about a year or so, then he started coming around again."

"How do you remember so specifically?"

"It's a family thing, once you're recognised as a family member then you're family."

"Was he always alone?"

"No, a few times he came with a tiny woman, oh skinny, way too skinny, always wore black, she even had black eyes." She was briefly interrupted by the arrival of a customer. "Victoria would help the customer please?"

"Sure auntie."

"She was bony," she continued, "needed a few good meals. They would have a coffee or two and then leave. She never smiled. He did, he had a really nice smile, handsome boy. I wanted to fix him up with my niece, but he never seemed interested."

"Do you happen to remember what they did? I mean, did they just drink coffee?"

Vicky Russo thought for a minute rubbing her hands on her apron.

"Once they were looking at photos. It was the only time I ever saw her animated, she was gesturing and talking and pointing to people in the photos, old black-and-white ones, some colour. But I don't know who was in them. Does this have anything to do with the accident?"

"As I said Mrs. Russo, we just want to tie up a few loose ends. And you never saw her here alone?"

"No, I didn't."

"Thank you, Mrs. Russo."

"Sure, no problem. But if you want to talk to her she lives just a few blocks away, off Woodlands."

DC Miller's head snapped up from the notes she had taken. "She lives near here?"

"Sure, I saw her go into the flat one day a while ago."

"How do you know it was her flat?"

"She was taking out the garbage, you only do that with your own place, mind you that's the only time I've ever seen her around, other than here of course."

"Thank you very much, Mrs. Russo."

"No problem, and officer, any coffee you want to buy we offer volume discounts, so bring in your colleagues."

Later that afternoon, DS Ian Roberts and DC Laura Miller sat in his office exchanging information.

"Taking it all together, what does it mean?"

"Let's review what you've found out about Derek Lawson."

Laura opened her notebook. "Well, firstly it's difficult to verify that he was or was not Peter Lawson's brother without a DNA test."

"One way to do it, has Peter Lawson ever donated blood?"

"I've checked. No."

"Disappointing."

"Yes, but that would've made our job too easy," she smiled.

"Go on," Ian prompted.

"Derek Lawson grew up in Italy with the name of Derek Lawson Russo. He came to Scotland about five years ago, shortly after Peter Lawson left for the United States. For some reason he stayed and worked part-time here for less than a year, then records show he went to California, after that. He stayed until three years ago when he returned to the U.K. and stayed in London for about a year and then went to Italy for a short time, he then came back here. He doesn't seem to work very much."

"How does he live?"

"Has an income from family in Italy."

"Any relation to the Russo in the shop?"

"Yes, Mrs. Russo said that he was a distant cousin, she'd wanted to set him up with someone, apparently he was quite nice to talk to if a bit vague. He came in a few times with the mystery woman, they just sat and talked, she also said there were family type photos, the girl spoke mostly."

"I want to know who she is!"

"Unless we actually catch her I don't know what to do, she's been seen but no one really knows who she is."

"Well, she didn't just walk out of the sea like Venus! She was born somewhere and has parents. What about the address Russo gave you?"

"Oh, that was a good one. I went and asked in the neighbourhood and she didn't live there. One of the neighbours was on holiday for a month and they saw our mystery woman there, alone, sporadically going in and out, but only in that month."

"So we didn't find out where she lives?"

"No. Again, Ian, that would be too easy."

"What about Derek? Where did he live?"

"He lived on Argyle Street but didn't spend a lot of time there, and she was never seen there with him."

"So where did he go when he wasn't there?"

"He spent some time in the local library. The girls remembered him once again because he was good looking, and again sometimes seemed kind of vague. One of them tried to ask him out and he told her he couldn't, that he was married. But she never saw him with a woman."

"What else?"

"I'm still checking the neighbourhood restaurants, pubs and so on, to see if anyone else saw them together."

"Good, good. Here's what else I want you to look into."

"Stefan you can't stay cooped up in the flat all day long."

"I'm not cooped up, I'm just working from home today."

"What are you, my personal bodyguard?"

"Well, it is a body I do love to guard."

"Stop it, I'm serious."

"And I'm not?"

Em pushed him toward the door. "You've been here for three days and nothing has happened, you have surveillance outside and cameras - I don't even want to think about where the cameras are! Now go."

"How do you know I have to go anywhere?"

"I can tell, you've looked at your watch every five minutes for the past half hour."

"Alright, alright, I can take a hint. Never thought I'd see the day when I'm kicked out of my own house."

"Well now you are, and if you do then I can get some work done. If I watch one more movie —"

"Or play one more game of strip poker?" he asked raising his eyebrows while trying to look innocent.

She laughed. "Well I have to admit your games are fun," she replied then pushed him more firmly toward the door.

He turned, swept her up twirled her around before setting her back down. "I'm going, I'm going. Now, your phone is on? And charged? And if you have any issues?"

"Yes, yes I'm well protected, now go," and with a final kiss, Stefan was out the door.

Stefan headed down the stairs and toward the street door. The rain was coming down in a solid wall, and he thought of one of the comforts of a good car and used the remote to start the engine of his BMW to turn on the heat.

The explosion that followed blew the wreckage of the car down the street and the flames licked toward the tops of the buildings. Stefan's immediate reaction was to dive behind the shrubs in the front garden for a split second then standing up to survey the area and see if anyone else was on the street. Fortunately, it was quiet so the only reaction were the neighbors rushing to their windows.

Em, watching from the window, only saw the explosion before the sight melted before her and she landed on the floor.

"Em! Em! Emily!" Stefan cradled Em in her arms, ice-cold and pale. He gathered her up and, wrapped her in a duvet and settled her on the couch. Her eyelids fluttered and she slowly opened to reveal frightened eyes. Stefan knelt with a bourbon to her lips.

As her eyes fully opened and she saw him Em started to cry, the tears streaming down her face.

"God Stefan, I thought that was you! I couldn't see you for the fire!"

"I started the car from the hallway, and that's when..." he stopped.

"This is like a nightmare, one thing after another. Who is it? Is it her? And if it is what does she want? I don't know her!" Em hiccupped between questions and sips.

"We'll find out, don't you worry. I'd just feel better if I could get you out of here."

"I know I'm not making it easy, but I just feel safe here, and with you."

"Bloody good I'm doing. Some strange woman gets in and then my car goes to pieces."

"At least you weren't in it," Em said taking another sip. "Suppose we should call the police?"

"I don't think we'll need to, with that explosion, we're going to have everyone here."

Em leaned back and thought to just a few months ago when life had been so peaceful, and now it was just explosive, not just in terms of things blowing up, but the emotional turmoil and everything else.

Em looked at Stefan. "You know, I stayed in my flat because it was easy and safe and nothing could happen to me when I was there, and it was that way for a while, but you know I am beginning to realise that you just can't stop life from happening and whether it's out there, or in my flat or in here, it's going to happen. I guess I can't hide forever." Em sighed at the sudden epiphany.

Stefan laced his fingers with Em's and looked into her eyes. "No, and you don't have to hide. Emily, I love you and have from the first moment I saw you. I will be here for you as long as you want me to be, and you don't have to hide here, you can be and live wherever you want to."

"Oh Stefan, when I saw that car explode and I thought that I had lost you, it made me realise that I am falling in love with you. I think that's why I fainted." Em curled herself up and snuggled into his embrace, her head fitting into the familiar crook of his shoulder. And despite the violence of all that had gone before she felt at home and safe in his arms.

A moment later he felt his arm slightly damp. "What's this crying?"

"Just a little. I'm just happy to know that you're alright, and to think…" She stopped. "Anyway, I don't want to think of that."

"Tell me, my dear, what can you think of that gives you pleasure?"

"Palm trees and a sandy beach," she said.

"Go on."

"When I was a little girl we would visit the beach in California and stay for the summer, there were palm trees and we hung a hammock up. There were lunch picnics and midnight swims, and bonfires at night with marshmallow roasted on open fires, and we made smores."

"What's a smore?"

Em laughed. "It's a Graham cracker with roasted marshmallows and melted chocolate made into a sandwich and you eat them at the bonfire wrapped up in a warm blanket. Sometimes we'd tell jokes or ghost stories, sometimes someone would play the guitar and we would sing songs."

"Sounds wonderful."

"Oh it was, it was heaven for me."

Em was silent for a moment. "Go on tell me more," said Stefan.

"Oh there was a special time of year at the beach when the grunion would come in only late at night, and we would all line up with our buckets and only go up to our ankles and pick up buckets full of water and there would be the grunion all floating in the bucket. It's called a Grunion Run, except we are the ones doing the running. They are such tiny little things, way too tiny to eat, but that's just what we did for the fun of doing it. Then we would have sandwiches and hot chocolate."

"Do you miss it very much?" he asked

"I sometimes miss the sound of the ocean and the palm trees," she continued. "Remember, those are the happy memories of childhood."

"Still, I think it's wonderful. Do you think it's something that we might be able to share in the future?"

Em snuggled even closer into Stefan's arms nodding. "I have to say I don't think there is anything that would make me happier than sharing a beach and a moonlit night with you."

John looked up from his examination, it was the sample from Stefan's car. He grinned. "It's a match."

"I don't know what you're so happy about! We've got someone on a let's-blow-up-everything-we-can rampage."

"You know that it's not exactly that."

"Well true, but it is a mess. First, we didn't have it and now we have these components that for some reason we can't trace but they will combust in a nice fiery explosion."

"Now Mrs. Lawson gave us the chemical breakdown from the message from her friend in the states right?"

"Right."

"Well, that puts this Peter Lawson right in the middle of it."

"Kind of, he may have invented it, but who has the recipe for it? He died in California three years ago, and they're just starting to blow stuff up now?"

"Actually Will, we don't know that. We've had a few cases over the last three years that have been similar to this, that we didn't know exactly what the origination was."

"True."

"Well, say that this stuff has been around for a while and we just haven't gotten on to it because it's not used all the time and we are just overworked and haven't figured it out?"

"Maybe it wasn't perfected and that's what took Lawson out?"

"If that's true then he must have been working with someone over here. Maybe his partner was that mystery woman that some people have seen but no one has talked to and who cannot be found."

"John, let's get back into this, there has got to be a way to be able to track this, something we're missing."

"Okay, but Will everything we've found is just normal chemicals, not traceable."

"I'm not giving up."

"I know, I know, me neither."

Stefan never left the flat and Sarah had all but moved in during the next few days. Em and Sarah convened in the lounge during the mornings and Em had forbidden Tommy to deliver until the situation was resolved.

Stefan arranged for deliveries from the local store and spent hours locked in his office on the phone and the computer. In the afternoons he would come out for lunch and then they would review events of the day. This was how life was for three consecutive days. The news carried the story on the explosion and they also stated the news that Stefan had died. Thus, Stefan was confined to the house to lend credence to the story, as he could hardly be seen out in public after he had been so spectacularly killed.

Grayson and Alisa called for daily updates and were equally forbidden to visit. Sarah was warned every day not to return and she returned every morning.

"Peter and Derek were my cousins and Em is as dear to me as a cousin. I will not be forbidden to be here!" Sarah declared, stamping her diminutive foot for emphasis.

Stefan had thrown up his arms and just had one more surveillance team added to follow Sarah around.

"How is it that you can simply order so much surveillance?" Em asked.

"It's my sparkling personality," he replied.

"You are definitely charming, but even you have limits."

"Let's just say that I have several friends at my disposal, who happens to be well placed in the area of, well, watching people."

Em rolled her eyes. "Will I ever know all about of you?"

"I'm willing to give you the rest of my life for you to find out," he said and brushed her forehead with his lips as he went to the kitchen to make tea.

"How did you find this address, Laura?"

"It was a second lease under the name Peter Lawson. The neighbours didn't see much of him, but did recognize the girl, said she lived here on and off for the last three years."

The officers cleared the area and entered the tiny tenement flat. Going through the front door they heard a noise and then a faint pop and then the flames burst out from the bedroom. Any evidence they were looking for went up with it.

DS Ian Roberts sighed. "She is thorough this one. Just a slip of a girl and we can't find anything on her except the occasional clue which ends up evaporating in a chemical blaze."

He clicked on the phone. "James, I've got another scene for your guys to sift through."

"I know, I know she's starting to leave a trail of devastation behind her. Guess this ties it up, she was involved with Peter Lawson somehow."

"What were you thinking of?" Stefan worked to keep his tone controlled. "If it is this mystery woman, wouldn't following her have been a better idea? Now her place has gone up like so much Glasgow property recently."

"Mr Lundgren they thought she was in there and with the way buildings and cars have been going up lately…"

"But there is no real proof that any of this is her, I know she broke in but she could be part of …"

"Part of what? You know what you're saying doesn't make any sense. Why would she want to do this, it just doesn't make any sense?

"Who the hell is she?"

"We're not sure, people have seen her but she has a few identities and we have no fingerprints to run on her and in any camera footage she has a big hat on and the only thing people remember is that she is really thin and all in black. Not much help."

"What about her features?"

"Mrs. Lawson wasn't even specific about that. Come to think of it, we'll sketch her, then we can run it against the database."

"Good idea, have them come by later today."

Stefan left Ian Roberts office just as Laura Miller walked in.

"Can you send a sketch artist over to Stefan's house this afternoon and see if we can get something from Emily Lawson?"

"Sure. Found something interesting though."

"What? And please make it good Laura, I'm a bit peeved about this one."

"I was doing a bit of research on Peter Lawson's education, and I found that he went to the same University where there was an explosion while he was there."

"Really? Please, go on."

"He attended classes with a Professor in mathematics and seemed to spend some time with him. Lawson had gone off to do some research during the summer and while he was away there was an explosion and two students were killed. The professor was held responsible and went to jail, sentence commuted when he was found to be dying."

"Well, I'll be damned."

"Oh, it gets better. There was a young girl resembling this mystery woman who hung around the university at the same time."

"So who is she?"

"Well that's it, she attended classes and was registered, but it too was an alias, when she left the identity evaporated off the face of the earth too."

"Am I crazy Laura or is this woman imaginary? Does she live in a vacuum and come out occasionally to drive us mental? How many people are like this that just almost don't exist?"

Chapter Twenty-Six

E mily had settled down to work on a writing assignment. Every time she started to write however, the image of that woman came to her. What was it about her that seemed so familiar?

She stopped working on the writing and started a list.

When Derek first wanted to meet me, he said he was Peter. Why? When Derek saw me though, he said he was Peter's brother. Again, why? He was then killed. Accident? Why? Why was my room blown up? Why was Stefan's car blown up? Moira said she saw Peter leave with this strange woman, but it must have been Derek. The same explosive was used to kill Peter and almost kill Stefan, so what is the common denominator? Why now? Who is she? Who is this woman who seems intent on making my life a misery?

This keeps up, she thought wryly, *the neighbours will want them to move, and at the very least insurance will go through the roof, once it's fixed that is.*

Sarah arrived and made lunch. As they ate, she and Em reviewed the list of questions with no answers.

"Could it have something to do with Peter's research? Remember what Alisa said, that he was working on something that the government wanted a part of?"

What do we have in the papers? Em said pulling out the box.

"Looks like gibberish to me."

"Anything mathematical looks gibberish to you, anyway, they're formulas, but formulas for what?"

"Didn't Peter tell you what he was working on?"

"No, he said that there was a part that was dangerous and he didn't want to share anything with me that might bring harm. We mostly talked about his general research projects. There was only one that he didn't share, and you could be right, that's probably the one that's the problem. Let's find out a little more."

Pulling out her laptop Em started a search on Peter Lawson. It brought up articles on his death, as well as a biography on his education and academic life.

"Wait a minute, look at that," Sarah said and pointed to a small feature link about an explosion.

Reading the article aloud Em related that there had been an accidental explosion at the university, two students were killed and a professor was held responsible. But nothing about Peter, still, it was at the university he attended.

"Do you think he knew about it?" asked Sarah.

"Must have. It would've been his second year at the university. I wonder if he knew who it was? This is definitely an explosive subject."

Sarah rolled her eyes. "Leave it to you to have a corny thought. Bad humour, really bad humour."

"What else can I do? Seems there are things blowing up with great regularity these days."

"Speaking of things blowing up, how is Stefan?"

"He's fine and he doesn't blow up, he's in his office working. For a photographer, he isn't out very much. Actually, he hasn't been on an assignment since this started." Then changing the subject Em asked "What if those formulas are for the explosive? Then there's another link."

"But Peter wouldn't work on anything that would be violent or bring death," Sarah countered. "He was so anti-violence, anti-war, a pacifist."

They were interrupted in their conversation by the buzzer, and Stefan emerged from his office. It was a sketch artist to take down Em's description of the mystery woman.

Sarah was miffed that she had not been asked to do the sketch, but was mollified when Stefan assured her that it had to be in a specific format.

"Hrmmmmph!" came the reply.

Settling in the lounge, the artist asked Em questions: the shape of the face, eyes, nose, and so on, feature after feature. In a surprisingly short time, the artist had finished. "Does this look like the woman?" she asked.

"Wow, yes. "I didn't think that I'd noticed that much."

"It's surprising what the mind can take in in just a flash. When you try to describe it all at once it doesn't come out right, but when you take it slowly, feature by feature, it works."

Sarah was studying the sketch, despite the fact she never enjoyed drawing people as it never seemed to come out to her satisfaction, and this small fact she had not revealed to Stefan. However, she was interested in examining the details of this sketch.

"Em?"

"Yes?"

"Look at this. Look closely and kind of scrunch up your eyes."

"What?"

"Just try it"

"Alright." Em looked. "Oh my God. Why didn't I see that?"

Chapter Twenty-Seven

T hey held the meeting in Stefan's front room. James, Ian, Laura, Sarah, and Em.

Stefan started. "I've gathered you all here - to unmask the killer." He held his hands up apologetically. "I know, it's not funny, but I've always wanted to say that." He continued, "Through much persuasion, I have invited everyone here to figure out what to do next. She's going to make a move soon and we don't know what it is or when it will happen, and it is best to include the professionals."

"What do we know so far?" asked Sarah

"She knew Peter and Derek, and for some reason, she doesn't like me," answered Em. "And she was seen with Derek in the States and seen with him here as well."

Further contributions continued and soon a picture was built up.

"Peter had the formula to this new explosive, and it's likely that is what killed him. It has been used since his death, so the bit that was found in the safety deposit box isn't the only copy in existence." added Stefan.

"The woman in question attended the same university at the same time Peter was there. Also there is the explosion that killed two students. He was away when it happened, but the professor held responsible was one Peter had a mentoring relationship with, so we have a connection there." contributed Laura.

"We also have the connection that she was seen in California with Derek at the time of the explosion that killed Peter." added Em.

"Remember," said Sarah, "that Derek looked injured and this mystery woman was helping him at the time, and that Moira who saw this did not report or say anything." Sarah waited a moment then continued. "At some point, Peter had put the formula in the puzzle box and left that in a safety deposit box and made sure that it was paid for."

"The real question is why did she, if it is this mystery woman, and Derek wait until now to start this up?" mused Em before continuing, "I mean I've been here three years."

"Maybe she didn't have the formula, she had to find it again, but why would she? What is her reason - her motive for doing this? And if Derek was in this with her why kill Derek?" Stefan added to the growing questions.

"Well, let's hypothesise for a moment," said Ian who had been quiet through the review process. "Let's assume that it is her, as she is the common denominator. She must have been working with Derek for some reason. Remember he first said that he was your dead husband before changing his story? Could he have been after an inheritance?" This question was directed at Em.

"Peter did have money from his father and when he died it did come to him. But Peter was never selfish with money, if Derek was his brother then he would definitely have shared. I mean we had more than enough, and I make quite a good living from my writing. So that wouldn't have been a good motive."

"Alright, at least we've established something. It comes back to Peter."

"Peter wouldn't be involved in anything illegal," Em firmly stated. "If he was meeting with some government agency it would be for the good of... well, the good of something. He just wouldn't, he was always for peace, really anti-violence, anti-war. Maybe that's why he hid the formula, so someone else wouldn't get it? Remember it was in a safety deposit box inside a Chinese puzzle box, and as a matter of fact, everything has been hidden away in a safe place."

Em sat up. "That's it! He was hiding it to make sure no one else could get to it." With that came more questions. "But what was he working on that the government wanted to see him about? Maybe some way to be able to find this untraceable stuff? That would make the most sense," she spoke almost to herself.

"Well, we agree that at the bottom of it, is this chemical stuff that is untraceable?"

James, who had been silent throughout the exchange, agreed with Ian.

"Both Peter and Derek are dead and the only one left is the girl. What about the professor that was involved in the explosion?"

Laura spoke up. "Records show that he died shortly after being released from prison."

"So it does come back to the girl and her motive."

Em had been silent for a minute, she disappeared into Stefan's office but came back empty-handed.

"Sarah, do you remember the Chinese puzzle box that we found in the small secret room?"

"Yes, the one we couldn't get open?"

"It's gone"

"What!"

"Stefan, do you remember seeing it?"

"Not lately. What do you think?"

"Well, every box has had a part of the puzzle, what if this box had the last piece, another formula? It would make sense."

"So where has it gone?"

"Mystery girl, remember her visit here? She must have known about it and she took it."

"How would she know it was here?"

"Just think about it, she's known everything all along. She's the only one who has known this story from the start."

"Do you think she knows what's in the box?"

"Yes, I do, and I think that she may know how to open it. How did she get in?"

Stefan went out and brought back the plans for the building. Holding them out, he pointed to a false top in the ceiling where the attic was. There was a small opening that had been covered on each and every flat when it had been renovated.

"I thought I remembered something like this," said Stefan, "when the renovations happened it had to be done in every flat."

Em looked at him.

"I promise to explain later. Anyway, this is how she got in, and I've since taken care of it. So what do we do next?"

Ian and James leaned forward. "Well, we have an idea."

Stefan groaned. "Somehow I don't think I am going to like it."

They both smiled. "Oh we both know that you are really going to hate it." James added. "That was a perk for me."

They all leaned over the lounge table and began discussions in earnest.

Chapter Twenty-Eight

*E*m saw the door was partly open. Every fibre of her being said *don't be stupid, don't go in there,* but there she was, gently pushing the door open. There was no change in the rooms, the bedroom was still cordoned off and the other rooms still had smoke damage which would require quite a lot of work to get cleaned up. Even though she had been in the flat several times since it still hurt to see the bedroom so devastated.

"I'm in here Emily." The voice came from the kitchen, a woman's voice.

Em stepped carefully around the debris in the hall and into the kitchen where there was only smoke damage.

It was her. She was thin and small with an oval face, her lips, like everything, were thin, and she was all in black with raven hair and eyes so black they matched the pupil. The only colour was the streak of red lipstick, stark against her pale face. She might have once been attractive, but there was a hardness to her expression that removed any possibility of beauty.

"Have a seat," she offered.

Em sat in the chair across the table from her.

She poured a neat whiskey into a glass, pushed it toward Em and refilled the one in front of her.

She took a large swallow. "Peter always did have the best taste in drinks."

Em, still silent, pulled the glass toward her but didn't sip, she had always hated whiskey.

"Do have any idea how much trouble you have caused me?"

Em shook her head.

She ticked off her fingers. "First Peter, then Derek, then Stefan, and finally now you." The corners of her lips stretched into a smile that lacked warmth or sincerity.

Em rolled the glass between her hands to keep them from shaking. "Why?" she asked.

She leaned forward in the chair and put her arms on the table, staring at Em. "My father," she answered and leaned back in the chair again.

Em returned her gaze and wondered.

"Don't worry Emily, I'm not going to let you leave this world not knowing the reason for this. We've got all the time in the world. Go ahead, have a drink."

Em took a small sip and grimaced.

"Might as well get comfortable, we're going to be here for a while. Where shall I start with my story? Oh, it goes back aways. Shall we start with Peter and when I first met him?"

Em's eyes widened.

"Oh yes Emily, I knew Peter a long time before he died. Best start with my father. Do you know he was famous? Well, he was. He perfected an explosive material that was undetectable and could be activated with ordinary water, like nitroglycerin. It was a thing of beauty, and it was going to make us rich. But I'm getting ahead of myself."

She stopped to pour another whisky and waggled the bottle at Em. "Have a little more? No? That's fine, more for me. Anyway, my father was a professor at that nice little university just down the street. Mathematics, he always did love playing with numbers, and in his spare time, he would play with explosives. He loved to tinker, and since I was the only kid he got me into it too. I'm just like him you know, he was thin and dark, Italian both he and Mom. She left him when I was little but I remember her."

She stopped, poured another whiskey and swirled it in the glass, considering the amber colour. Her eyes were this colour and her hair was so long it went down past her waist. She closed her eyes for a moment and then opened them to look at Em. "But I take after my dad, small, dark and good with explosives. Peter was one of Dad's students. Dad mentored him and worked with him, and then when —" She stopped and her eyes narrowed. "It was an accident, an accident!"

She leaned back in the chair glaring at the quiet Emily for a moment then the rest of her words came out in a rush. "Dad had been working the in the lab at the university and some of the chemicals were exposed, and those stupid kids weren't supposed to be there, and because of their stupidity, my father had to pay! He lost his job, his work, his freedom, his will, and then his life, all because of those stupid kids! And what did Peter do? Do you think that he helped? Spoke up for my father? No, he didn't, and it broke my heart. So it was only just that he paid the way my father paid."

She stopped again and looked at Em with hatred. "I loved him first. I would have done anything for him, but he thought of me as a kid, and then he left and went to California, and I stayed. Took me a while to find him because he was supposed to go to Australia for a special project."

She leaned forward again. "Do you know what the project was? It was to find the chemical formula to be able to trace the explosives my dad had invented, so not only did he *not* defend my dad, he left and then was going to block the only thing that my dad had done in his work!"

She took another swig of the whiskey. "I have to admit, the first time I saw Derek I almost choked, damn near killed the wrong guy, to begin with, but here I am getting ahead of myself again."

She focused on Em again. "Not drinking?" she asked. "Don't you trust me? I wouldn't either if I were you. But don't worry, I'm not going to put you out. I want you wide awake so you know when the end is here. Oh, don't think you can escape now. I put a release on the door so that once you walked through it anyone that comes in, or out of it, will also be blown into tiny little pieces."

Em shivered.

"Oh yes, I put a whole lot more in this batch than I put in your bedroom. Actually, if I do say so myself it's enough to take out this entire side of the building, and maybe a little bit more."

Em watched her consume the last of the drink and couldn't believe that she showed no signs of being drunk. *What to do? Was it really true? It had to be her that killed Peter and Derek and thought she had killed Stefan. She clearly had nothing to lose, but Em did, and she wasn't going to go out like a lamb.*

"Where was I?" she asked as she poured yet another drink. "Come on, you're way behind."

Em took another small sip to appease her and finally spoke. "When was the first time you met Derek?"

"Oh, about five years ago. He had come looking for Peter, they really were twins you know?"

Em nodded

"Derek had the test done from a tooth or something. Anyway he came here looking for Peter and I ran into him down in that intersection you so love to watch," she sniggered.

"He had tracked down Peter from the family that owns The Coffee Cafe, some kind of relatives. Anyway, he was looking lost and I thought it was funny that he didn't know me, so he explained who he was, and I just kept staring at him, the Italian accent coming out of Peter's lips, too weird. So I spent some time with him and eventually told him that Peter was in California, and he wanted to go right away, but I convinced him to delay going while I worked on my plan. You see, I had just found Peter myself and wanted to map it out just right, so I didn't want Derek going in and spoiling it all. And I do clean up fairly good, it's harder now though, I'm too damn skinny." She frowned and for a moment Em felt sorry for her, she had lost so much.

"Don't go feeling sorry for me," she said, reading the emotion on Em's face. "Feel sorry for you." She rubbed her knuckle on her left hand with a massaging motion and then stopped to down the drink.

She pulled up the handbag from the floor, rummaged around and pulled out a photo and slid it across the table to Em.

"So Emily, which one is it?"

Em looked at the photo of the girl with Peter, a curvier, softer, more beautiful version of the woman across from Em now.

They were both smiling and Peter's hair was ruffled. His face, with a few days' stubble, couldn't hide the dimple in his chin. Em's heart skipped a beat looking at his face. For all the changes lately, he still had that effect on her.

"They were both good-looking, weren't they?" she said and slid another photo, this one with the girl and Derek, and although they were identical, Em could see a subtle difference. It wasn't so much in the features as it was the expression. Peter was always open and smiling, whereas this picture was more reserved.

"I guess you can tell the difference?" she asked and Em nodded.

"So my original spark of genius was to have Derek and Peter meet and then replace Derek with Peter so I could get my hands on Peter's new formula. It is worth a fortune, the explosive is good, but if it can be traced then that is worth so much more." She smiled and her thin lips curved up then down again.

"But the timing was off, Peter got blown to bits and Derek ended up hurt, hit on the head, and it was all I could do to get him out of there and back here."

Em looked confused.

She rolled her eyes. "I needed Derek to think he was Peter, and the best way to do that was to get him back here and into Peter's life, which would have worked except you showed up and hibernated in this damn flat. I couldn't get in here. So it took longer because I had to spoon-feed Derek, and he kept getting confused when his memory started coming back and interfering with the memories that I was giving him, supplied with all the photos, and history and visiting all the places Peter had been - I gotta admit, I got a bit carried away, it was a way for me to have a life with Peter." She looked directly at Em. "Since you took him away from me. So Derek was my substitute, Peter. It wasn't so bad, Derek was good in bed and seemed to be happy."

Em looked at the clock, which read 3 am. Stefan was due back at about four. She suddenly felt her phone vibrate in her pocket and hoped the vibration wasn't audible or visible.

"I might have lived that way for a while," the woman across the table continued, "except he walked down that intersection you watch all the damn time and he saw you, and dammit if he didn't fall for you too! What is it about you anyway? Does every man that meets you fall in love with you? I mean, first, you had Peter hanging on your every word then you have that stupid photographer across from you traipsing after you for three years, and then Derek! Give me a damn break, it was too much!"

Em took another small sip and rested her right hand on her lap under the table, the left holding the glass.

"Since Derek was starting to get confused with his memories, I suggested he work on meeting you. That's when he talked to your little red-headed messenger boy, then that Swede lost his temper and hit him."

"So why did Derek change his story when he came to see me? Why didn't he say he was Peter and go along with your plan?" Em asked.

"His memories had been coming back slowly and I didn't know much, so just to be on the safe side I put a little bug in his pocket. Apparently, when your boyfriend hit him it jarred something loose because all his memories came back and he decided to come clean with you. He wasn't going to tell me and I got a bit mad and —"

"And you ran over him with a car." finished Em.

"Yes, stolen from around the corner. Thought that it would get your boyfriend in hot water, but he has some serious friends in all the right places."

"But why?"

"Because he was no use to me, to tell you the truth, and I didn't know what else he would say if he would blow the whole scheme, and he must've thought you wouldn't believe he was Peter who was dead back in California, and if he was himself he could still get close to you but on his own terms, not mine. So he was no longer of any use to me, whatsoever."

Em turned slightly in the chair and pulled the phone out of her pocket and put it on her lap, never moving her eyes from the woman across the table.

Once again she poured a drink and this time she splashed more into Em's glass. "You really do need to drink more. What is it, you don't like whiskey?"

"Not really," said Em.

"I've always loved it. I could drink Peter under the table, that's where I got the taste for it, now it has its other benefits. Do you know how my father died? Crippled up in a wheelchair until he finally couldn't get out of bed. They had released from prison finally, at least he didn't die there, he died at home, and guess what?"

Em looked at the strange woman all in black, with such white skin and black circles forming under her eyes. "What?" she asked quietly.

She started laughing. "It's hereditary! Ain't that a laugh! I am my father's daughter. But I will not die crippled up in a wheelchair."

Em's eyes widened

"Doctors say I could last for years," she continued, "but that's no life for me. It's getting bad enough, anyway, that's not important. What is important is that you hear the entire story before you get yours. Where was I again? Ah yes, good old Derek. He was history and now I was left with no easy access to this place, with you in hibernation and me having to figure out a contingency plan. It wasn't too hard, I just plonked a little explosive in your grocery order, the part that would make it into the bedroom and then waited. I did hope that you would be here when it happened and it would have killed two birds with one stone so to speak, but it was fine, either way, it would get you out and then I could get in. But I'll be damned if you didn't move that stupid trunk before I could get into it. How did that happen anyway, Emily?" Her eyes narrowed as she waited for a response.

Em related the story of how Sarah had brought back the key with her from California.

"Yeah, I'd forgotten about that, but I didn't think it would find its way back here. Unbelievable, it's all about timing I say. So that caused me another delay. Now, do you understand what patience I've had with all this waiting and then being circumvented?"

"How did you know the trunk was gone?" Em asked.

"Oh, I had made a little visit and that's when I left a little more of the explosive."

"Why?"

"Easy, if they thought that it was unstable then they might clear out the whole place and then I could see where the trunk was because I didn't think it had left, I figured it was somewhere close. But you kept staying here and he kept staying with you and then those two rookies came in, that was great, I was laughing so much I thought I'd end up rolling on the street. Anyway, that was two down, and since your boyfriend wasn't moving I had to arrange a little accident to get him out of the picture and then I knew you'd be next."

"But why Stefan?" Em persisted.

"Don't you get it? Because he was here and so were you and I wanted in that trunk. If I got rid of him then you'd have to leave there, it's not your flat, you don't have any right to be there, then I'd have a chance to search, find what I wanted and then go after you. But actually, this is going to work better for me, because I have what I want." She reached into her bag again and pulled out the Chinese puzzle box that Em hadn't figured out how to open.

"Do you know what's in here?" she asked from across the table.

Em shook her head.

"It's the formula to track my father's explosive. It's the only one in existence and once we've gone up it won't be in existence any longer and my father's legacy of the untraceable explosives will live on. You never would've figured out the box," she said.

Em agreed. "I got all the rest but I couldn't get that one. Will you share what it is?"

"Yes and no."

Em tilted her head.

"Yes, I'll tell you what you probably already know he always used names to open the boxes. "It's a name, Peter always...

Yes, I thought that, but I couldn't figure this one out.

"No, and you never would have. You see, it's my name," and she pressed several parts on the box and it opened.

Inside was a memory stick and a miniature photo, the same one she had shown to Em a short time ago of Peter and the girl.

"He did love me you know," she said and looked up at Em. "Just not the way he loved you."

Realizing time was growing short Em asked again, "Why is it that you have to kill me?"

"Why not? You are such an irritation to me. You had Peter and then when you lost him you spend your life holed up in this flat, and you still manage to have these men fall in love with you, Derek and your precious Stefan! Even that little red-headed brat drops at your feet."

Em shook her head. She had thought that if she stayed in this flat, her home, the home that Peter had designed for their life together, that she would be protected and she wouldn't have to go out into the world that had taken so much from her, and now, here the world was invading her home. She wasn't any safer in here than she would be out in the world, and here she was calmly discussing her life with the woman who had essentially caused her to be here - the irony made her smile. This was the woman who had murdered at least two people and thought nothing of ending Em's life as well as her own.

Em gulped down the last of her drink and set it on the table.

"Finally," she said as she poured out nearly the last of the whiskey. "Once it's done, so are we."

"And there's not much left," said Em. "What is your relation to Peter and Derek?" she asked.

She looked at Emily and raised her eyebrows. "Good one. I'm a distant cousin. That's why it was so bad when Peter wouldn't come forward for his own family. I looked more like them before I got so skinny, the face loses something."

"And the heart," added Em.

"What do you know about heart? What have you lost? Oh, I know Peter died but he wasn't supposed to be there. I killed him, but I didn't mean to, I just wanted to scare him so that he would give me the formula. When he saw his lab destroyed and he knew it was me, and then how would he be able to get out of being blamed when he was seen leaving the area? You see I had thought it all out, and it all went to hell when he got killed. I couldn't find the damn formula and he was dead! No use to me." She paused to look at Emily. "The open signal on your phone won't help, no one can get in here now."

"Oh, I beg to differ with that statement," said Stefan, who had materialised behind her."

"What the hell!?"

"Surprised to see me?"

"You went up with that dam car!" she screeched.

"Not quite. I have this handy little device that lets me start it remotely, which I like to do in cold weather, and it was freezing cold that day if you remember."

Stefan had snapped handcuffs onto her wrists, but she didn't struggle.

"It doesn't matter now you stupid bastard. You're in here too and you're not going to get out," she smirked.

"Why not?"

"Because when your little girlfriend came through the door and closed it that set the seal for the explosives. This entire house is sealed in, anyone trying to get in or out goes to pieces," she laughed

Em frowned, a look of consideration on her face. *What if I didn't close the door? It really couldn't be that simple*, she thought.

"What if I stepped through it and left it open?"

"No, you closed it, I heard you."

"No she didn't," said Detective Roberts, holding up his phone. "Nice work Mrs. Lawson."

She slumped in the chair.

"I am arresting you in relation to the murder of Derek Lawson and also the attempted murder of Stefan Lundgren and Emily Lawson you are not obliged to say anything, but anything you do say will be taken down in writing and may be given in evidence. Do you wish to say anything?"

She shook her head.

"Before you take her away I'd like to ask her something?"

"Go ahead."

"Did you mean to kill Peter or was it really an accident?" Em asked.

She looked at Em. "I loved him, and hated him for what he didn't do for my father, but I couldn't have killed him. You, on the other hand, I would happily kill, because you have so much and don't even know it or appreciate it."

Em looked at her. "That's where you are wrong," she said. "So very wrong," and Em took Stefan's hand. "I know exactly what I have and I do appreciate it."

Over the next few days, the formulas were compared and since one negated the other, they were sent for filing with the government to be destroyed or filed away, whichever seemed like the best way to get rid of it.

Sitting in the lounge a week later, Em asked Stefan, "How did you know that she would try what she did?"

"It just kind of made sense. She was after you and wasn't going to stop until she got you, and against my better judgement Detective Sergeant Roberts persuaded me that the only way to catch the cat was to use a mouse — you my dear, were the mouse. I wasn't going to take any chances, so I had a crew come in and take out the boiler and it left enough room for me to hide out in there. Roberts wasn't too crazy about that, but it was the one thing he could not change my mind on."

He reached out to stroke her hair, "if anyone is going to be there for you it's going to be me." A moment passed and then he continued, "I'm sorry I didn't tell you, they were afraid she put a bug in the place that we couldn't find, and if she knew it might provoke her into doing something rash, although none of her violence was guns, she just used cars and explosives."

"What will happen to her now?"

"She's being held over for trial."

Stefan's phone buzzed. "Hello… She what?... She did what? Well, I'll be damned. So what do we do now? That means we're in the same boat as before."

He hung up the phone. "I don't believe this. She had some kind of fit or something so they took her off to the hospital, where she managed to escape as some kind of orderly assistant or something."

"So she's out?"

"Yes."

Em laughed and Stefan looked at her as if she were nuts.

"You have to admit, she is persistent. Besides, I have to say that through all of this I do feel different. So the question is what do we do now?"

"Just sit tight for a few hours and let's see what happens."

"I have a question."

"Yes?"

"What would you like for lunch?"

"Dessert first."

It only took a few hours before the final answer came through.

Stefan turned to Em. "It's finished," he said. "It's over. She went to a different flat and was apparently making some new explosives when it went off, there was a fire, no survivors."

"No one else was there?"

"No, it was a small block of flats and they were all out."

Em walked over to Stefan and straight into his arms. "I can't believe it."

Chapter Twenty-Nine

" Gosh Em," Tommy said as he scrutinised another chess move. "I can't believe all this, it's just like one of those action movies."

Another few days had passed and Tommy had been allowed to start doing his errands again. Work had also started to restore Em's flat.

"I have to say that it was quite exciting, and you were a great little detective, going to the shop and finding out what you did."

Tommy blushed. "Oh, it was no big deal and it was kind of okay because, well…"

"Yes?"

"Because I got to know Victoria better and she's really nice, and I'm teaching her chess."

"I see," said Em smiling.

"Oh, don't worry Em, I'll still play with you. Nice to have someone else to practice with."

"Of course, of course."

"Will I bring extra stuff for Sarah tomorrow?"

"No, I don't think so. Sarah has gone off to California to visit friends and do some painting, and I think she'll be gone awhile."

Actually, it may be quite a while, Em thought as she remembered the conversation.

"Grayson and Alisa insist that I stay in the west wing of the house, as they're going to be doing some travelling. I'm also going to be helping out their chauffeur Al, you know he's an art student?"

Em recognised the tone and the smile on Sarah's face. "That is so good of you, does he show talent?"

"Oh yes, he does."

"And…?" Em stretched out the word.

"And, well, he's nice to look at, and eager to learn about art and the last time I was there we had a pleasant talk about it."

"How old is he?"

Sarah blushed. "Twenty-three."

"Oh, he's only four years younger, that's not bad at all."

"He's going for his degree and he's serious about his art, so I'm just going to help a bit."

"And it doesn't hurt that he is young and handsome and will probably fall at your feet, as they all do!"

Sarah laughed. "Probably, but there's something different about this one. Anyway, we'll see."

"Em! Em!"

"Oh, sorry Tommy," Em snapped out of her daydream, "is it your move or mine?"

"Yours, and then I have to go. Mrs. McLean has an order for me and I need to go to the store to get a new lead and collar for her cat."

Over the candle-lit dinner, Em and Stefan talked about the past but still didn't go into the future.

"Guess who stopped by today?"

"Only heaven knows," said Stefan.

"Detective Constable Laura Miller."

"Really, and what did she want?"

"Well, she asked how I was doing and how I felt about everything that had happened. She's a nice young woman."

"And…?"

"And it turns out that her younger brother is agoraphobic, doesn't go out at all. So we had a chat and she gave me a card of a counsellor who specialises in people with this.…I think it's referred to as a disorder, well whatever it is called there is something I can do about it, and I guess talking about it is the best way to start."

"My ears are all yours…and everything else too." Stefan said with a slow wink.

"You have my ears, my lips, and… my love." Em replied with an even slower wink.

Epilogue

*E*m stood at the window and looked out at the intersection below. So many people with so many stories. The kid on the bicycle, and the young couple walking side by side with just their fingers touching. A few children on their way to summer school and the woman with shopping bags filling her arms. Em's gaze followed each of them until they were out of sight. As always, each one had a story in her imagination.

Stefan came up behind her, gently wrapping her up in his warm embrace. "It's a nice morning out there, and we have the whole day to celebrate Mrs. Lundgren."

She smiled and turned around, looking up at him. "Actually, the graduation ceremony is not until tomorrow, but you know I love a good celebration, by the way I think you might properly address me as Dr Lundgren." She turned back to view the ocean and asked. "What do you think about a walk along the beach my love?"

"I thought you'd never ask," he said, pulling her more closely into his arms.

Suddenly the french doors to the bedroom burst open.

"Mama!"

"Daddy!"

"Mama!"

"Daddy!"

Both Stefan and Em were barrelled into by two blond children, the smaller was a girl with curly hair, the larger was a boy with straight hair flopping on his forehead, and both with brilliant blue eyes.

"What is it?"

"What is going on?"

Both children held up the iPad with a small announcement. ***Grunion Expected to arrive by Midnight Tonight.***

"Well, I don't know," began Stefan.

A chorus of Ohhs and excuses and reasons began the assault.

Em laughed, "You might as well give in, it is a majority rules, and I agree with the children."

Em turned to view the vast ocean and back to her family, "we have time for one quick swim and then both of you need a nap if you want to stay up for a grunion run."

"Yahhoooooo" in chorus again, as they ran to change.

Stefan rolled his eyes and smiled. "Well if the grunion are running we had better go catch them, before we head back home to Glasgow, as I know for a fact there are no grunion in Glasgow."

Em lovingly tapped his nose with her finger, "I have to say I think I have the best catch of them all, here or Glasgow, or anywhere in the world." Then left to change into her suit for a swim in the ocean and all the life that beckoned outdoors.

About the Author

Catherine Grace was a journalist, wrote computer tutorials, and worked international corporate events, however her creative outlet was always writing stories. This novel is her second publication. The reason she selected Jasami Publishing Ltd to assist with her first publication is that it aligned with her personal ethos, to give back to the community. Catherine lives in Scotland.

Other Books By This Author

For The Latest Information On

Available Novels

New Releases

&

Coming Soon

Please Visit

JasamiPublishingLtd.com